THE SECRETS OF GHOST ISLAND

>>MAX & ME MYSTERIES>>BOOK 3

THE SECRETS OF GHOST ISLAND

PATRICIA H. RUSHFORD

MOODY PUBLISHERS
CHICAGO

Cover Design: Studio Gearbox.com
Cover Photography: Steve Gardner / PixelWorks Studio
Interior Design: DesignWorks Group (thedesignworksgroup.com)
Editor: Cheryl Dunlop

ISBN-13: 978-0-8024-6255-8

We hope you enjoy this book from Moody Publishers. Our goal is to provide high-quality, thought-provoking books and products that connect truth to your real needs and challenges. For more information on other books and products written and produced from a biblical perspective, write to:

Moody Publishers
820 N. LaSalle Boulevard
Chicago, IL 60610

Printed in the United States of America

To Madelyn Marie,
My great-granddaughter—
What a delight!

AUTHOR NOTE

It may seem strange to some that I would choose heroes like Jessie Miller and Max Hunter—one with leukemia and the other living with an abusive aunt and uncle. I suppose it's because I have cared for children who have suffered and even died with life-threatening illnesses and have worked with children tormented with emotional and physical pain at the hands of abusive adults.

These children were so often brave and resilient and able to overcome great adversity. They showed me what being a hero is all about. As a pediatric nurse and then a counselor, I have always had a heart for children and a desire to help them in any way I can. My earlier nonfiction books *Have you Hugged Your Teenager Today?* and *What Kids Need Most in a Mom,* were written to help and encourage parents in their endeavor to better care for their children. *It Shouldn't Hurt to be a Kid* helps parents, teachers, and caregivers to recognize abuse and to help bring healing to broken children.

Several years ago, I began writing *The Jennie McGrady Mysteries* for kids because I love a good mystery and according to the fan mail I receive, so do kids. My goal has been to provide great, exciting, and adventurous stories, but also to empower kids to rise above the problems they may encounter in life. Jessie and Max do this very well. I hope my readers and fans will enjoy their adventures as much as I have enjoyed writing them.

With Love, Patricia Rushford
www.patriciarushford.com

CHAPTER ONE

A scream tore into my dream, ripping it away and snapping me awake. Another scream. Then another. My heart dropped like a skydiver without a parachute.

Max, what have you done this time? I'm not sure why I immediately thought of Alice Maxine Hunter, my best friend. But why else would the girls be screaming in the middle of the night? I supposed it could have been a murderer or something, but I doubted it. We live on a quiet street on the banks of Chenoa Lake in the Cascade Mountains. Even with all the tourists we get, the crime rate is low. Though considering the events of the past few weeks, not everyone would agree.

Porch and yard lights popped on outside at least four houses, including mine. My dad had taken time to put on his jeans and a T-shirt, but he was barefoot when he came outside. He stopped by the porch swing where I'd dragged my sleeping bag an hour earlier.

"Jessie, are you okay?" Dad hunkered down beside me.

"Yeah, but I don't think they are." I nodded toward the frantic girls bouncing around on our neighbors' lawn.

He ordered me to stay put, so I did, while I watched the adults try to put some order into the chaos. Fortunately, the yard lights had nearly turned the dark night into daylight, and I could see just fine from where I was.

"There's a snake in my sleeping bag!" Jamie Carlton's high-pitched wail broke as she jumped up and down.

"There's one in mine too!" That shrieking voice belonged to Emma Keith.

The third victim's terror had already turned to rage. Sunshine Dougherty had straddled Max's sleeping bag and was throwing punches at what was probably Max's head. "You did this, didn't you? You . . . you . . . vagrant!" My dad pulled her away from the bag and led her to one of the lawn chairs around what had been our campfire earlier that evening.

"What's going on?" The voice came from the open patio door behind me.

"Aah!" I nearly jumped out of the swing. "Max! What are you doing here?" I glanced back over at the lumpy sleeping bag on the lawn. "You're down there getting your face punched in."

"Obviously not." She yawned and sat down beside me, setting the swing in motion. "Seriously. I heard screaming. What's going on?"

"Come on, Max. You can quit pretending like you don't know. You put snakes in their sleeping bags."

"Snakes? No kidding." Max grinned, revealing the small gap between her front teeth. "How cool is that?"

"That was mean." A small giggle slipped out of my own mouth. "Funny, but mean."

"You think I did it?"

"Didn't you?"

"No. Not that they didn't have it coming. Those three are the worst." Max's grin grew wider. She looked over at me and must have seen the doubt in my eyes. "I didn't do it, Jess. I swear. Besides, when would I have gotten the snakes?"

She had a point. We'd been together most of the day before going to Ivy Cavanaugh's sleep-over party. I'd been afraid something like this would happen. Ivy had invited all of the sixth-grade girls to her party, and some of those girls hated Max and me. Well, maybe *hate* is too strong a word. Let's just say they didn't associate with us unless they were forced to. Like at Ivy's party.

The party had been okay except for Sunshine, Emma, and Jamie being total snobs and not speaking to Max and me. Even with that we'd had a good time. Max was right; the girls did deserve some payback. But if she hadn't done it, who had?

"What are you doing up here anyway?" I asked. Just a couple of hours ago, we'd all stretched our sleeping bags on the lawn.

"Couldn't sleep. I came in to get a glass of water." She eyed my sleeping bag. "What about you?"

"I couldn't sleep either. The ground was too hard on my bony body, so I decided to sleep in the swing."

"Don't look now, but the posse is headed this way."

I cringed. "This can't be good." My dad, Ivy's parents, and the less-than-happy party girls were heading straight for us.

Jamie, Sunshine, and Emma started yelling at once, all of them accusing Max. Ivy tossed me an accusatory look as if I'd had something to do with it. I splayed my hands in innocence.

"Max?" Dad folded his arms. "Would you care to explain?"

Max shrugged. "I didn't do it. I wish I had."

Sunshine started up the deck stairs, probably aiming to throw a few punches at the real Max.

"Hold on, Sunny." Dad caught her and told her to stay back. "Max just said she didn't do it."

"Then it was Jessie. One of them put snakes in our sleeping bags."

Max had way too big a smile. "I wonder why you'd feel that way," she said. "You think you might have done something to deserve it?"

"I'll get you for this, Hunter. Count on it."

Why her parents ever called her Sunshine, I'll never know. She didn't live up to her name—that's for sure. Okay, I'm prejudiced because of the way she acts toward Max and me. I have seen her bright side, but right now she looked more like a thundercloud.

"Just calm down. No one is *getting* anyone." Dad turned back to me. "Do you know anything about this, Jessie?"

I started to shake my head when I heard a giggle and a shush coming from under the deck. "Maybe." I pointed downward.

Dad nodded and hunkered down by the open side of the deck. "I might have known. Sam Miller, you and your friends come out of there right now."

"You're busted, Sam." Max chuckled.

My five-year-old brother emerged first, followed by the twins, Brian and Benjamin Davidson, from next door. "But Dad, we din't do nothin' wrong," Sam insisted.

"We didn't," the twins echoed.

"Where did you get the snakes?" Dad asked.

"From our snake pit under the tree house," Sam said. "It's to keep imposters out."

"You mean trespassers?" Dad was trying to keep a straight face, but I gotta tell you, with Sam it isn't easy. He's a funny kid. I just hoped he wouldn't get into too much trouble with the snakes.

"Yeah, trespassers."

"Would you like to tell me why you put snakes in the girls' sleeping bags?"

Sam pointed at Sunshine. "They were mean to us. We just wanted to play with Deeogee and they made us go away."

Deeogee is Ivy's boxer. He's this crazy dog that swallows cakes whole and eats candy with the wrappers still on. I could hear him barking from inside their house where he'd been banished earlier in the evening after tearing open a bag of marshmallows.

"They were being pests." Sunshine still had her hands clenched. "It was a girls-only party."

"You weren't even having the party yet." Sam glowered at her. "'Sides, they were just garter snakes."

"You little brat." Sunny, which is what most of us call her, would have throttled all three boys if it hadn't been for the adults.

After Dad made the boys apologize, Carly Davidson signaled for her twin sons to follow her, lecturing them on sneaking out at night. She didn't mention the snakes, but I imagined she would when she got them home.

Ivy's dad sighed. "Okay, everyone. Party's over."

"Sam, go up to your room," Dad ordered. "We'll talk more about this in the morning."

Max gave Sam a thumbs-up sign that Dad didn't see. Sam signed back. I had a hunch Max wasn't as innocent as she claimed to be. She may not have put the snakes into the sleeping bags, but she might have just happened to mention the idea to Sam as a practical joke.

Things settled down after that, and everybody went back to bed. Ivy and her friends picked up their sleeping bags and went back to Ivy's house, where they decided to spend the rest of the night inside. Max and I decided to stay on the porch at my place. Like Ivy's dad had said, *the party's over.*

Once things quieted down and the lights went out, I was ready for some serious sleep. Max conked out about the time her head hit the pillow, so I couldn't confront her about the practical joke. Not that I minded much. Those girls deserved it.

I lay there for a while thinking about Sunshine Dougherty and her followers. I called them that because whatever she did or said, the other girls, especially Emma and Jamie, did. Ivy used to hang out with them all the time, but in the past couple of months, she's been around them less and she's been nicer to me. Maybe because we're neighbors and used to be good friends before I got leukemia six years ago. She changed after that. Or maybe it was me who changed. Chemo made me lose my hair, and I wasn't the nicest person to be around. Besides all that, Mom pulled me out of school and homeschooled me until this past year. With being sick and not going to public school, I didn't really hang around with any of them. Not that they would have wanted me to. I didn't fit in.

I ran my hand over my still-bald head. Tears filled my eyes, and I brushed them away. *Do not feel sorry for yourself, Jessie Miller. You don't need friends like Sunny. You have Max and Cooper.* Cooper Smally had been one of the mean ones when I first went back to school, but we've been friends ever since I rescued him from Bear Island. Okay, I didn't exactly rescue him—I just told the sheriff where to find him.

Sunny and her gang have never liked me, but they didn't start being total jerks until I became friends with Max. I thought about Sunny pounding Max's sleeping bag and calling her a vagrant. That seemed strange to me. Of course, the way Max dressed in baggy thrift-store clothes, she sometimes looked like she lived on the streets. I think the real reason Sunny doesn't like Max is that she can't bully her. I can understand Sunny being upset about the snakes, but I don't remember her ever being so angry. She looked like she could have killed Max.

I pushed my thoughts and feelings away. I didn't like the fact that Sunny and her friends wanted nothing to do with us, but it wasn't worth losing sleep over. Besides, Max and Cooper were much more fun to hang around with. And much more forgiving.

Instead of thinking about Sunny, I gazed up into the star-sprinkled night sky and then took in the rest of the view. The full moon sent a shimmering path across the water, making it look like a magical wonderland. The lake looked as calm as a lily pond.

Someone in a rowboat cut a swath across the moon's image, disfiguring the scene. I sat up and rubbed my eyes, thinking I must be imagining things. I was about to wake Max when a cloud covered the moon. The darkness swallowed the boat and the rower.

Must be a camper, I decided. It wasn't all that unusual for people to boat to the islands and spend a night or two. But this late? Why not wait until morning? And where would they be going? I could have been wrong, but it had looked as though the boat was headed for Ghost Island. I stared out at the water for a long time but didn't see the boat again.

Ghost Island is about two miles northeast of our dock. The island is an ancient Native American burial ground and is off limits without a permit. Anyone going there would be breaking the law unless they were granted special permission from the government. I could see a faint outline of the island along the south shore. For a moment, I thought I saw a light flicker. Maybe my imagination or my tired eyes were playing tricks on me. *Or not.*

I burrowed deeper into my sleeping bag, trying to ignore the goose bumps on my arms and neck. Ghost Island was definitely not a place I would want to row to in the middle of the night.

CHAPTER TWO

The warm sun and voices coming from the dock woke me the next morning. Sam and Dad were taking the boat out. It's one of those lightweight aluminum boats with oars. It has a small motor on it now in case someone rows out too far and can't get back. Dad got the motor after my unplanned trip to Bear Island, on the far side of the lake.

The fishing poles told me all I needed to know. I imagined Dad would have a heart-to-heart talk with Sam about the snake incident last night. I'd been in on a few of those talks, but not nearly as many as Sam. Fishing and hanging out with Dad always made the usual parent/kid lectures easier to take. Getting to my feet, I stretched and yawned. Dad and Sam waved at me from the boat.

I almost stumbled over Max's sleeping bag, which she'd already rolled up. I hurried inside, wanting to tell her about the rowboat I'd seen last night. Only she wasn't there. "Where's Max?" I asked Mom, who was sitting at the table in the bay window drinking her coffee.

"Amelia picked her up a few minutes ago." Amelia Truesdale was Max's new foster mother. More like a grandmother, really. Amelia is 79. You'd never know it though. She owns Lakeside Farm, the lavender farm just outside of town, and makes all kinds of crafts to sell.

I frowned. "She could have at least said good-bye."

"Amelia had to come in early to run some errands. Max asked if she should wake you, but I told her to let you sleep. You haven't gotten enough of that lately."

"Thanks a lot." I hate when Mom gets overprotective like that. I pulled a box of cereal out of the cupboard and grabbed a bowl out of another, and then shut the doors harder than necessary.

"Lose the attitude, Jessie, or you can forget about going anywhere today."

Like I have anywhere to go. Without Max, life could be incredibly boring. After getting milk out of the fridge, I sat down at the table. "Sorry," I said, mumbling a halfhearted apology.

"Hmm." Mom set the newspaper down and brushed a hand through her thick hair.

"What?"

"There have been two more robberies. One the night before last. And I saw on the news this morning that another house was hit last night up in Lakeside."

"I didn't know there had been any," I said. But then I hadn't exactly been reading the paper or watching the news.

"The first one happened a week ago. Two houses in Steamboat

Landing were robbed last weekend. Thursday night the Summerfields got hit. That's too close to home."

"What was stolen?"

"The paper has a list of things. Credit cards, money, iPods, cell phones, jewelry. Small things that are easy to carry."

Small enough to fit into a boat? I wondered.

Mom brought me my medicine and a glass of water. "Don't forget your pills."

"I won't." While she started on the dishes I ate my granola and read the article. The Summerfields lived about a block away from us. Steamboat Landing had the nicest houses in the area. It was a gated community, and all the houses faced the lake. Sunshine Dougherty and her parents and her older brother live in Steamboat Landing.

"It's scary to think someone was burglarizing the neighborhood while you girls were sleeping outside last night," Mom said. "We've had a false sense of security around here for years."

"Do the police know who did it?"

Mom shook her head. "They seem to think the thieves are tourists."

No surprise there. The police blame the tourists for everything.

"Whoever they are, they're very adept at getting in and disarming the alarm systems."

Scary is right. I was about to tell Mom about the boat I'd seen on the lake last night when the phone rang. Mom answered it and handed it to me. "It's Cooper."

My heart flip-flopped. Maybe the day wouldn't be a total loss after all. "Hey, Cooper, what's up?" I pushed my chair back and headed upstairs to the privacy of my room.

"Something big. I need to talk to you and Max right away."

"Sure, but Max isn't here."

"I know. She's at the farm. How about I pick you up and we row over to get her?"

"Dad and Sam are using our boat."

"Okay. I'll bike out to the farm and we can use Max's canoe. We'll come get you."

"Where are we going?"

"I'm not sure yet. Someplace where we can talk privately."

I hesitated. "I'll need to check with my mom."

He gave me his cell phone number. "I'm leaving right now. Call me if you can't come."

I said I would, then went back downstairs to find Mom. To my relief, she agreed to let me hang out with Cooper and Max, but only after I'd brought in the sleeping bags and straightened up my room. I gave her a hug. "Thanks. You're the best."

She laughed. "Just be careful and . . ."

"I know. Don't overdo." I'd only been out of the hospital for a little over a week from having a bone marrow transplant. I still felt weak sometimes, but so far everything seemed to be going okay.

"And wear a hat. Here, catch." Mom tossed me the floppy denim one. It wasn't the most fashionable hat in the world, but it was soft and lightweight. Most of the time I didn't bother with a head covering, but in the summer I had to wear a hat or a scarf to keep from getting sunburned.

After pulling on capris, a T-shirt, and shoes, I straightened my room and put away the sleeping bags from the porch, and then grabbed my backpack. After I'd slathered sunscreen all over myself, I threw the tube in my bag. I also tossed in a notebook and pens in case I needed to take notes. Downstairs, I grabbed some snacks —apples, granola bars, and baby carrots—and put them in a separate bag and stuffed those in my backpack too. Unplugging the cell phone from the charger, I slipped it into a side pocket. The only thing left was a jacket in case the weather turned cold.

By the time I got down to the dock to wait for Max and Cooper, I felt like I needed a nap. I wouldn't take one, of course. Cooper had me curious, and I had no intention of staying home.

Being tired is what frustrates me most about having leukemia. Well, that and needles. Hopefully the bone marrow transplant will cure me—at least for a while.

I'd only been on the dock a couple minutes when I spotted them rounding the bend. Even with the life jacket, I was nervous about getting into the canoe. Rowboats at least have a flat bottom and are not so easy to tip over.

After they eased up to the dock, Cooper held the canoe steady while Max took my bag and helped me get in. They'd saved the spot in the middle for me, and I appreciated it. "I hope you guys know how to paddle this thing." The canoe wobbled from side to side until I got seated.

"Piece of cake," Max assured me.

Cooper chuckled. "Just don't make any sudden moves."

For the next few minutes I sat perfectly still, keeping a white-knuckled hold on the sides of the unsteady canoe. After a while, as they rowed farther away from shore, I began to relax.

"Where are we going?"

"Just far enough so we can talk without anyone hearing us." Cooper had a tight set to his jaw.

"Must be serious."

"You might say that."

I still couldn't believe how much Cooper had changed this summer. Right after school let out, he and his dad went to a camp in Oregon to trim down and get healthy. Before that, Cooper had been nearly as round as he was tall. Since school let out, he'd grown at least two inches and lost about forty pounds. He looked amazing with his dark hair and blue eyes, and you could actually see his muscles. They were straining now as he pulled the oar, taking us farther and farther away from shore.

As houses along the shoreline grew smaller, I could see why they would appeal to burglars. It looked as though the people living there had tons of money. Most of the houses were newer and bigger than ours. I thought ours was perfect—partly because my dad designed it and had it built. We inherited the land from his parents; it's been in the family for a hundred years. Dad says there's no way we could afford to buy land around the lake these days.

The houses stopped at the edge of a new development right where Amelia Truesdale's Lakeside Farm began.

Max poked my shoulder. "There's Amelia." She waved at the woman standing on the dock. Amelia waved back and lifted up a mess of trout.

"I didn't know she fished."

Max laughed. "I think she does everything."

Cooper pulled the oar up and laid it across his lap, dripping water on my arm. The cold water felt good. I almost wished I'd packed a swimsuit, but the water's too cold for swimming unless you're close to shore. As the canoe drifted, Cooper told us his news and I understood why he'd been so upset. "Enrique's missing."

CHAPTER THREE

The news about Enrique Sanchez didn't surprise me too much, but it did make me feel incredibly sad. Enrique was our age and went to school with us. He was one of the quiet kid, and I didn't know him very well. He didn't mix much with the other kids, but I knew he and Cooper were good friends. I hadn't seen him much since school let out for the summer. In fact, the last time had been at his dad's funeral.

Carlos Sanchez had worked for Amelia Truesdale. When Carlos went missing, everyone thought he had run away because he was an illegal immigrant. It turned out to be more than that. Carlos had been murdered. I won't go into the details, but he left Enrique and his two little girls behind. At the funeral I wondered what would happen to them. I knew they were staying with their aunt, but only until the authorities could locate relatives in Mexico. Their mother had died about four years ago when they were still living in Mexico. An accident, I think.

Cooper had lost his mom a few years ago too—to breast cancer. I had a feeling that was one of the things that drew Cooper and Enrique together.

Max and I waited for Cooper to give us details.

"All I know is that he didn't want to go back to Mexico." Cooper sighed. "I talked to him a couple of days ago, and he was really worried. I guess they have a grandmother there, and the authorities are going to deport him and his sisters. Their Aunt Leah is a citizen and she's been trying to keep them with her, but the immigration people say the kids have to go back."

"That's not fair." Max glanced at the mainland. "Can't we do something? Maybe Amelia can—she knows everybody."

Cooper shook his head. "My dad says the government isn't going to budge. There are too many illegal aliens in the country as it is, and they're not about to figure out a way for the kids to stay."

"Do you know where Enrique went?" I slipped my hand into the icy water, lifted up a handful, and let it waterfall off.

"No. All I know is what was on the news last night. Enrique and his sisters disappeared. Their aunt said they'd gone to bed the night before, and in the morning they were gone. She says they ran away to keep from being deported. They don't want to leave their friends."

"He took his sisters with him?" That worried me. The girls were younger—Callista was nine and Maela, five.

Max rolled her eyes. "He couldn't just leave them, Jess. The immigration jerks would have taken them. Think about it. If you were in Enrique's place, would you leave Sam?"

"No, but they're so young." I sighed. "What can we do?"

"That's why I wanted to talk to you guys," Cooper said. "See, I'm thinking you and Max have done some pretty cool detective work lately. Face it—without you, the cops would still be looking for those bad guys you caught. Between the three of us, we should be able to figure out where Enrique is, and maybe we can bring them food and stuff they need. The only thing is, you have to promise not to tell the police."

Max and Cooper both looked at me. "Or your parents," they said in unison.

I flinched. They were both referring to the time I told my mother that Max was being abused when she wanted me to keep quiet. "But they can't stay in hiding forever. Callista and Maela are too little to be on their own."

"Jessie." Cooper leaned forward and acted like he was talking to a little kid. "It won't be forever. Just until his aunt can figure out a way to keep them here."

I'm not good at keeping secrets from my parents. Maybe because we're so close and I've always felt like I could go to them for everything. I trust them to do the right thing, and they usually do. I wondered what they would say if I told them about Enrique and his sisters. Would they be on our side, or would they agree with the immigration authorities?

"Okay," I heard myself saying. "I won't say anything for now, but if something bad happens, I'm telling my folks."

"Deal." Max leaned back. "Anyway, it's too soon to worry about that. We haven't found them yet." She seemed pretty sure that we would. I wish I could have been that confident.

"Right," Cooper said. "We can't say anything about looking for them though. We need to be careful what we say and who we talk to. The police already questioned me. I'll bet they talk to all the kids who went to school with us."

"What did you tell them?" I asked.

"The truth. Enrique didn't tell me anything."

"So where should we start?" Max's tone had risen a couple of levels while we'd been talking, and I could tell she was getting excited. My own heart was beating a little faster, but I didn't know if it was from excitement or fear. Working against the authorities wasn't exactly on my list of good things to do. On the other hand, we'd be helping three desperate and scared kids.

"I'm thinking we should start by talking to the aunt." Cooper started rowing again, dipping the paddle into the water on one side, then the other.

"Perfect." Max smiled at me. "Relax, Jess. We're doing the right thing."

I wasn't so sure about that, but I nodded anyway.

You're probably thinking I'm a big chicken, but I'm just cautious. Or at least I try to be. I suppose it comes from being sick so much and having to be careful about everything I do. Max just jumps into things, like diving into the lake. I have to go more slowly—like testing the water first. "Do you know where Enrique's aunt lives?" I asked.

Cooper nodded. "Enrique lived there before his dad was killed. I guess they moved in with her when they came here from Mexico. She's Carlos's sister."

"I never met her. Carlos used to come to our church and bring his family. That's where he met Mrs. Truesdale. I didn't know about their aunt until the funeral."

We headed back to our dock and got there just as Dad and Sam were coming in.

I can't tell you how embarrassed I was when we got back to my place. My mother insisted on feeding us lunch, which was fine. But she also insisted that I take a nap. "Mom," I said through gritted teeth, "we have plans. I can rest later this afternoon." *I'm not a baby,* I wanted to add, but didn't.

"It's okay, Jess," Max said. "Your mom's right. You should rest."

"Yeah. We'll wait for you." Cooper didn't seem to mind. "We need to go back to the farm to get our bikes anyway. We'll come back and get you before we . . ."

"Go into town," Max finished.

What could I do? I hate being ganged up on, but to tell the truth, I felt supertired—especially since I hadn't slept much last night. I picked up my pillow and quilt from the big basket by the patio door and walked outside with Max and Cooper. While they ran down the bank to the boat dock, I stretched out on the swing. Part of me wanted to run after them, but the more reasonable part of me knew that my mother was right. I did need to rest. I just hoped they wouldn't go to visit Carlos's sister without me. I fell asleep trying to put myself in Enrique's place. Where would I go if the authorities were after me? Where would I find a safe place to hide with two little girls?

CHAPTER FOUR

I woke up when I heard the patio door open.

"Hey, sleeping beauty," Max greeted. "It's already two o'clock. You've slacked off long enough. It's time to ride."

"Ride . . . ?" I mumbled. "Where to?"

Of course, the answer came to me before the question completely left my lips. *To see Enrique's aunt.*

"Leah Estrada," Max said. At my questioning look, she added, "Cooper and I did a little detective work. We have her address and even called her to make sure she was home."

"Wow. I'm impressed." I folded my quilt and stuffed it and my pillow into the basket just inside the door. After making a trip to the bathroom, I met Max and Cooper in the driveway. Cooper already had the buggy hooked up to his bike. The buggy wasn't exactly the ride I'd had in mind.

"It's a ways," Cooper said when I started to object. "North of Lakeside. You might as well save your energy for later."

"Besides," Max said as though she'd read my mind, "we don't want you to have to call your parents to come pick you up."

"Okay." I reluctantly climbed inside. Just so you know, I don't like being ferried around in a bike buggy. I would rather have taken my own bike. Unfortunately, I can't ride very far. More than once I've had to call my parents to come get me because I didn't have enough strength to make it back home. What Cooper and Max had planned made more sense, so I leaned back in the seat and watched Cooper do all the work.

It took us twenty minutes to reach Leah Estrada's house. It was in an older neighborhood in Lakeside. Some of the houses were run-down, but most of them had been kept up. Unlike some of the newer places, there were some gargantuan trees and shrubs. Several rhododendrons near the house almost obliterated the windows. We rode up the narrow sidewalk and stopped.

Leah came outside before Max and Cooper had even gotten off their bikes. "Cooper, I am glad to see you." Leah had long black hair pulled back in a large barrette. She looked my mom's age.

Cooper introduced Max and me, and we followed Leah inside. The house had seemed small from the outside, but inside it was comfortable and neat. On one wall was a kind of shrine. A small table held a fake stone archway that stood about two feet tall and a foot wide. Tucked inside were a crucifix and a statue of Mary. The rest of the house was bright and cheery. Leah had used a lot of red, yellow, green, and blue decorations to accent her beige furniture.

"Would you like something to drink?" Leah asked. "I have iced tea, sodas, or milk."

Max and Cooper asked for Cokes, but I just wanted water. We

sat down in the living room and waited. Looking around, I thought how crowded it would have been with five people living there.

A few minutes later, she came back carrying a tray of cookies and drinks. Sitting down with an iced tea for herself, she asked, “You told me on the phone you wanted to talk to me about Enrique. Have you seen him? Do you know anything?” She spoke with a slight Spanish accent.

“You speak good English,” Max said. “Better than Carlos.”

Leah smiled. “I was born here. My parents immigrated to this country thirty-five years ago. My accent comes from always speaking Spanish to my family.”

Cooper cleared his throat. “We haven’t seen or heard from Enrique. We were hoping you could tell us something. We’d like to look for him and his sisters.”

“There is so little to tell. Like I told the police, I woke up yesterday morning and they were gone.”

“What did they take with them?” I asked, hoping that would give us a clue. I already had an idea, but didn’t want to say anything yet.

“Their backpacks for school are gone and some books. Crayons and coloring books. I think Callista took things for little Maela to do.”

“What about food?” Max’s gaze swept the room.

“Some snacks are missing and some fruit. There is only enough food to last two, maybe three days.” She looked hopeful.

"Maybe Enrique will come back here for more."

"I doubt that," Cooper said. "The police will be watching the place."

Max frowned. "So the cops know we're here now? What if they followed us? They might think we know where they are."

"Which we don't." I glanced out the front window. "I didn't see any police on the way here, and I don't think they have enough officers to have someone watch the house all the time."

"You're probably right." Max picked up a couple of cookies.

Leah set her tea down on a coaster. "She is right, Max. The police are looking for them, but I don't think they are making the children a priority. They are more worried about the robberies being committed against those rich people in the big houses on the lake. The immigration authorities are only interested in finding the children so they can deport them."

"I don't understand. Isn't there an Amber alert?"

"Yes, and I am sure the police are trying to find them, but we are Hispanic."

"Prejudice." Max pursed her lips.

"That is partly true," Leah said. "There are many bad feelings about immigrants. Some people are more than happy to be rid of those who are not like them. Not everyone feels that way. The newspaper reporter who came to interview me about the children seemed sympathetic. He said he would make sure the information got out to the television stations in Seattle and in Oregon."

"We had a debate about the immigration issues at school."

Cooper leaned forward, resting his elbows on his knees. "About half the kids think there shouldn't be any sanctions and that illegals should just be sent back where they came from."

"I remember." Sunny was one of them. She thought the police should round up all the illegal immigrants in the country and deport them. I wasn't about to tell Leah that. "I'm not sure how I feel about it," I added. "I want people like Enrique and his sisters to become citizens and not be deported. Some of the laws don't seem fair, but . . ."

"We have laws to protect our country." Leah nodded. "It's a very complicated issue, and unfortunately, we are not going to solve the problem today." She smiled and looked at her watch. "I need to go to work. One of my homemakers didn't show up."

"We'll look for Enrique and the girls." Max stood. "How can we get hold of you if we find them?"

She handed Max a card that read *Leah's Homemaking Services* on it in dark letters. "My cell phone is there."

"My mom has used your company," I said. "Sometimes, when I'm really sick, she brings people in to clean and cook. I don't remember ever seeing you."

"I have ten homemakers working for me." She sighed. "In fact, the police want to question all of my employees and me about the robberies. We do a lot of our business in those expensive neighborhoods. Since my homemakers are given keys and security codes, we are all suspect."

"Even you?" Cooper opened the door, and we stepped outside.

She hesitated and gave us a wry smile. "I'm afraid so."

"I have one more question," I said. "If the authorities deport Enrique and his sisters, where will they go?"

"Their mother's parents live in Mexico City. The grandparents love them very much, but they are old and poor and barely able to take care of themselves. It would not be a good situation. Carlos was hoping to become a citizen, but he was killed before he could make it happen." She shrugged. "Enrique said he would not go back." Tears filled her eyes. "He said he would die first, and I'm afraid that could happen."

We left Leah's house, but I didn't know where we were headed. I had climbed into the buggy without asking Max and Cooper, and they hadn't told me. Maybe they didn't know either. All I knew was that I felt heavy inside, like I'd swallowed a ton of lead. I was worried about Enrique, Callista, and Maela. I felt angry that the police weren't doing more to find them. Angry that our government would send three children, who had friends and family and a home here in the United States, to a place they didn't want to go. I prayed that they would stay safe and that we would be able to find them. Then I worried about what we would do if we *did* find them. Who could we tell? How would we be able to help them?

CHAPTER FIVE

We stopped at the Alpine Tea and Candy Shoppe for something to drink. They have my absolutely favorite dessert there, chocolate-dipped strawberries. They also had cool air. The outside temperature had climbed to 85. I felt sure the sunscreen I'd put on this morning had dripped into my shoes. I took my hat off and wiped the sweat off my forehead with my arm.

Ivy was working and seemed glad to see us. I was still finding it hard to accept her friendship. She whispered something to her mother, who smiled and nodded. The three of us, Max, Cooper, and I, sat down at one of the round tables. Ivy came right over. "You guys look hot. Must be pretty warm out there."

"Very," Cooper said. "I'll have a blackberry Italian soda. Use sugar-free syrup. No cream."

"Good choice." Ivy grinned, her cheeks pinker than when we'd come in. Though she hadn't said anything to Max or me, I was pretty sure she had a crush on Cooper. By schooltime next year I imagined a lot of girls would feel the same way. Cooper didn't seem to notice.

Looking at me, Ivy said, "Let me guess: chocolate strawberries."

I grinned. "I'm too predictable. Bring six and we'll share them."

"Nice." Max chuckled. "I want raspberry Italian *cream* soda."

I ordered lemonade. When Ivy brought our order, which had two extra strawberries, she went back for a plate of shortbread cookies and lemonade for herself, then sat down with us. "I hope you don't mind if I hang here with you. I need a break."

"Sure," Cooper said. I think Max minded, but she didn't say anything.

"I wanted to apologize for the way Sunny acted last night." Ivy snatched up one of the cookies. "She's been in the weirdest moods lately."

"It wasn't your fault," I said. Max kind of snorted.

"She's not usually so . . . well, so . . ."

"Violent?" Max finished.

"Um—yeah, I guess. Mom thinks it's because her parents are selling their house."

Max grinned. "You mean they're moving? Like out of state?"

I kicked Max under the table and hoped she could read my be-nice message. Just because Sunny is nasty there's no reason Max had to be.

"I'd be upset too." Cooper picked up one of the berries and bit into it.

"Well, all I know is Emily went to her house yesterday and Sunny had been crying. You all know that Sunny does not cry." Ivy shrugged. "Emily said she might have gotten in a fight with Jason."

"Who's Jason?" Max asked.

"Her brother," I answered. To Ivy I said, "I thought he was going to the University of Washington."

"Me too," Ivy said. "All I know is something strange is going on in that family."

I ate a strawberry, but it didn't taste quite as good as it should have. I didn't think I'd ever feel sorry for Sunny, but I did.

"Do you guys want to go swimming this afternoon?" Ivy asked. "I get off in an hour. I could meet you at the pool."

Chenoa Lake has a big community pool, but I've only been there a few times. My mother worries about bacteria like *E coli*. According to her, even though the public pool is treated, it's not a safe place for me to swim.

"I'm good with that," Cooper said. "What do you guys think?"

"Fine with me." Max sipped on her drink. "In fact, I think that's a great idea."

"Sounds like fun," I said, "but I'll have to check with my parents." The look on Max and Cooper's faces told me they had something in mind besides swimming. My guess was that they planned to talk to the kids who were there to see if anyone had any clues about where Enrique might be.

"Even if you can't swim," Max said, "you can hang out with us and put your feet in the water."

"Great." Ivy snagged a cookie and pushed the plate closer to Cooper.

Maybe I'm paranoid, but on the way home I began to wonder about Ivy's eagerness to get us to the pool. Even though she'd been nice to us, I didn't completely trust her. I mean, what if she had some kind of revenge planned against Max because of the snake thing? When I mentioned this to Max and Cooper, they didn't seem too worried. "What are they gonna do, Jess?" Max asked. "It's a public place, and there are lifeguards."

Mom wasn't too excited about the pool idea, but decided it would be okay as long as I didn't put my face in the water. "Since you're going, would you mind if Sam went too? He's been bugging me all afternoon to go swimming."

"But Mom," I groaned.

"Jessie . . ." Mom tossed me a warning look. I knew the next words out of her mouth would be, *If you don't take Sam, you can forget about going.*

I gave up. "Okay. You guys don't mind, do you?"

"Hey, I'm cool with that," Max said. "Sam's my bud. Where is he?"

We found Sam in the backyard playing with the twins, who wanted to go swimming too. Half an hour later, all six of us were in the van waiting for Mom to finish talking to the twins' mother, Carly.

I spent the next two hours sitting around in whatever shade I could find, watching about fifty kids play in the water. I'm way too skinny and don't like wearing a swimsuit, so I kept my towel wrapped around me. When I got too warm, I slipped into the shallow end of the pool to cool off, and then got right back out.

I talked to some of the kids from school, but most of them didn't even know that Enrique and his sisters were missing.

Ivy didn't show up. Sunny and her friends were there, but true to form, they ignored Max and me. Her occasional sneers told me she was still out for revenge. When nothing bad had happened by the time Mom came back to pick us up, I figured I'd been imagining things. Max and I headed for the showers. It felt good to wash away the chlorine, and I stayed under the water for a long time.

"Hey," Max yelled. "Where's my towel?"

I grabbed for the hook where I'd hung my towel, but it wasn't there. "I knew it was too good to be true," I muttered. It turned out Sunny and her friends had taken our towels and our street clothes. We were stuck in the locker room with absolutely nothing to wear except our swimsuits.

Hearing our screams, my mother came in. Though she didn't exactly laugh, she wasn't feeling sorry for us either. She handed Max and me some damp towels she'd taken from the boys, then went to find our clothes. What she came back with were rags. Sunny—I knew without a doubt it was her—had cut and ripped our tops and shorts into sheds. By now, Mom was furious.

"The war is on," Max grumbled as we followed Mom out to the van. "Just wait until I get my hands on those girls."

"It w-won't do any g-good." My teeth were chattering, and I was so cold that my goose bumps had goose bumps.

"Don't you want revenge? We can't let her get away with this."

"I j-just want to g-get warm."

When we got home, I saw Ivy watering the flowers in her front yard. She acted like she hadn't seen us, which made me think for sure she'd been in on Sunshine's little clothes-stealing game from the start. I felt used and angry. So much for us being friends.

Max and I hurried up to my room. Mom loaned her a sweatshirt to put over her swimsuit while I changed into some warm clothes.

Cooper was waiting for us out on the deck. Even though he thought the practical joke a mean thing to do, he seemed to think it was pretty funny. He was, however, more than happy to help us plan our revenge.

He and Max stayed for dinner, which gave us some time after we ate to go back out on the lake and talk about our next step in finding the Sanchez kids.

"Did you guys talk to anybody at the pool who knew where Enrique might have gone?" I asked.

Neither had. "I have some ideas," Cooper said. "If I were running away, I'd get on a bus and head for someplace in western Montana."

"Why Montana?" Max pulled up her oar.

Cooper shrugged. "I like Montana. There's some good fishing there."

Max rolled her eyes. "Enrique wouldn't have had enough money to buy bus tickets, and he wouldn't risk hitchhiking."

"For sure." I nodded. "Somebody would probably pick them

up and take them straight to the police." I looked around. "I'd hide right here on the lake. Remember Bear Island? Now that's a good place to hide. All of the islands around here would be."

"I agree," Cooper said, "but it would take us days to search even one island."

"What about Ghost Island?" I told them about the boat I'd seen cutting across the water the night before. "I can't be sure, but it looked like that's where it was heading. And who would be going out there that time of night unless they were hiding?"

"You are brilliant, Jessie." Cooper looked at me like I'd just given him a million dollars. "Pick the one island that's off-limits. Ghost Island has to be the first place we look."

My face felt hot, but it wasn't from the sun.

Max fastened her gaze on the island. A misty fog had moved in from the northeast and settled around it, making it look as spooky as its name. "I vote we sneak out tonight and have a look."

I swallowed hard and rubbed at the sudden goose bumps on my arm. "We won't be able to see anything. And we could get lost."

I thought she was going to call me a wimp, but she didn't. "Tomorrow's good." I couldn't tell if she was just being nice to me or if she had a few doubts of her own.

Cooper leaned back with his hands behind his head. "We can head out after church. We can meet here at like 10:30." He arched an eyebrow and looked at Max, then me. "What are you going to tell your parents? They'll want to know what we're up to."

"Just that we're exploring the lake. They'll be okay with that." I hoped that would be the case.

"Mrs. T will too."

"Good. My dad loves when I'm active."

"Okay. How about we bring a lunch?" Max suggested. "That way we can stay out on the lake longer."

"Sure," I said, trying to keep the worry out of my voice.

Cooper and Max dropped me off at my house at 8:30. Within an hour I was sprawled out on my bed trying to go to sleep. I wasn't afraid to go to the island. Okay, maybe I was—a little. Maybe a lot, because all night long I kept telling myself that the legends I'd heard about spirits inhabiting the island were just made up. Like the one about the Indian princess named Chenoa. And yes, the lake was named after her. She'd gone fishing with her brother and gotten lost on the island. They'd searched for days, but Chenoa was never found, and sometimes late at night if the wind is blowing just right, you can still hear her weeping. Her father named the lake Chenoa to honor her.

I think some of the stories are true, just not the ghost parts. Hundreds of years ago, there really had been a tribe of Native Americans living on the shores of the lake. The old ones went to Ghost Island to die, and it was where they buried their dead. Settlers came and transmitted diseases like small pox and cholera. The natives died out, and the few who were left moved on. No one knows how many were taken to the island.

All we know is that the archeologists who come there to dig

are always finding important artifacts. A few years ago, one of the archeologists died during a dig. Some people say the spirits killed him. Some say he died of natural causes. No one really knows.

I groaned and turned over, covering my head with a pillow. *Jessie Miller, you have to stop thinking about this stuff. You don't even believe in ghosts.*

Okay, so maybe I do, just a little.

CHAPTER SIX

The next morning after Mom woke me up for church, I took a ten-minute shower just to wake up. To be honest, I thought about calling Max and telling her I couldn't go, but I wasn't about to let Cooper and Max go to Ghost Island without me.

Max and Cooper were supposed to meet at my house at 10:30. They were there fifteen minutes late and came by boat—canoe, actually. "Sorry we're late," Max said as she balanced on the rocking canoe and jumped onto the dock. "Cooper came out to the farm to help me with chores. Then Mrs. T fixed us a big picnic lunch."

I probably shouldn't have let their time together that morning bother me, but it did. Fortunately, I didn't say anything stupid or snooty. I was jealous of their time together without me, but more than that, I resented my illness and having so many limitations.

"I need to go back inside and get my stuff." On the way to the house, I tried to adjust my attitude. *You are lucky to be alive, Jessie Miller,* I lectured myself. *Enjoy what you can do, and don't be angry about what you can't.*

Though Mom had told me the night before that I could go, she recited her usual warnings and had to go through her list. I covered myself with sunscreen and remembered to grab a hat.

"Be sure to drink lots of water so you don't get dehydrated," she called from thc patio. "And if you get tired, come home."

"I will." I waved back at her, happy now to be going out on the lake with my friends.

Dad thought it was great that we were exploring, but insisted we take the rowboat with the motor instead of Max's canoe, in case we got into trouble. I was more than pleased with that arrangement.

Mrs. Truesdale had packed a picnic basket for us, and the wonderful smells coming from it made my mouth water. Cooper set it in the front of the boat under Max's seat and put the blanket I'd brought over it. Dad handed him the small cooler with pop and water in it.

"We have enough stuff to last a week," Cooper complained as he helped me in and handed me my backpack.

Dad laughed. "That's what happens when you let women do the packing."

"At least we won't run out of food," Max said.

"Remember to just use the motor for emergencies. There's plenty of gas, so you should be fine."

"Hopefully we won't need it. I'm working on strengthening my arm." Cooper got in and shoved off. Without asking, he set the oars in place and started rowing. Cooper had broken his arm a couple of months ago. The cast was long gone, and he seemed strong as ever. Though they hadn't said, I imagined he and Max would take turns. Maybe I'd try rowing some too.

"You okay, Jess?" Max studied my face. "You look kind of pale."

"I'm fine." I ducked my head. "Just tired. I was too excited to sleep." *And too scared.* I kept the last part to myself.

"Yeah." Max leaned back, apparently glad to have Cooper row. "Me too. I asked Mrs. T about Ghost Island." She laughed. "You should have heard the stories she told me."

"Did she tell you about the Indian princess the lake was named for?"

Max nodded. "I'll bet you've heard them all."

"Probably." I turned around to look at Cooper. "How about you?"

He frowned as he pulled on the oars, lifted them, and pulled again. "I've heard a lot of things. They're stories, that's all."

"Have you been on the island?" I asked.

"A couple of times. Dad and I went on a dig last year. It was cool. I found some arrowheads, but we couldn't keep them. All the artifacts people find have to go to the museum. Everything found here belongs to the Indians."

"Bummer." Max dipped her hand in the water and splashed some on her legs. "You couldn't keep anything?"

"Nope. But my dad has a collection of arrowheads that he got when he was a kid. They didn't have all those rules then. Don't tell anybody though. He could get into trouble for even having them."

It took us nearly an hour to row out to Ghost Island. As we got closer, I recognized a familiar scent. "Is it my imagination, or am I smelling a campfire?"

"You have a good nose, Jessie." Cooper leaned forward and sniffed the air. "That's exactly what it smells like."

"I don't see any smoke." Max twisted around so she could see better.

"Maybe it's on the other side of that hill."

"One thing for sure—someone has been here."

"Unless it's the ghosts," Max said. Ghost Island was about a mile in diameter. Though it wasn't a perfect circle, it was close.

As Cooper rowed closer, I started getting worried. "We're not getting on the island, are we?"

"Not yet. I thought we'd row all the way around it." He put both oars in the oarlocks. "Max, would you mind switching with me? My arm's hurting pretty bad."

"Sure. No problemo."

I held my breath while they maneuvered around me. "Just don't tip us over."

They managed to switch seats and sit down. Once the boat stopped rocking, I started breathing again.

"The island looks a lot bigger close up." Max shaded her eyes and looked up at one of the high rock formations.

"Go to your right." Cooper directed Max with a wave of his hand. "There's a sandy beach and a dock up ahead. Maybe we can tie up at the dock and eat."

"That sounds good," Max said. "I'm starved."

The towering rock wall gave way to a sloping, tree-studded hill that eventually settled into a sandy cove. The dock Cooper had talked about reached out into the deeper water. I was surprised to see a boat twice the size of ours tied up there.

"Someone's here," Max said.

"It can't be Enrique." Cooper frowned. "He wouldn't leave a boat in the open like this."

"I agree," I said. "I'll bet there's a dig. Look at the University of Washington insignia on the boat."

About that time a guy came walking out of the rustic-looking bathroom at the base of the hill. He spotted us right off and waved as he jogged toward the dock. "Hey, Kev," he yelled in the direction of a large tent. "We got company."

The guy was young, blond, tan, and well built, with glasses and a sloppy-looking hat that matched his khaki shorts and camouflage T-shirt. College student. Archeologist.

"Whoa," I heard Max mumble. "He's hot."

"Hey, kids," he greeted. "What are you guys doing out here?"

"Um—just looking around," Cooper told him. "My dad and I were in on a dig out here, and I wanted to show Max and Jessie." He tossed a rope onto the dock. "We weren't expecting to see anyone."

"Kevin and I got here last week." He grinned as he tied the boat to the piling. "I'm Josh Morgan, by the way."

"Cooper Smally." Cooper took Josh's hand and stepped out onto the dock. He introduced Max and me as Josh helped us onto the dock too.

Josh glanced back toward the tent. "My buddy and I were just breaking for lunch. Would you like to hang with us? We can show you some of the artifacts we've found if you're interested."

"Sure." Cooper reached into the boat for the picnic basket and cooler.

"That would be great." I jabbed my mesmerized friend in the side. "Wouldn't it, Max?"

"What? Oh, yeah. Cool."

We followed Josh through the sand and up a short footpath to their camp. Josh moved one of the flaps aside. "Kev, you in here?"

"Where else would I be?" Kevin sounded gruff but managed to smile at us when he emerged from the tent. He had at least a couple days' growth of facial hair and looked kind of mangy.

"You'll have to forgive Kevin. My friend doesn't do well without his beauty sleep. And we haven't had much of that this weekend."

I perked right up at that. "Why?" I asked, wondering if it was their boat I'd seen on the water Friday night.

"Partying mostly. But then you kids wouldn't know about that." Josh winked at Cooper.

"Did you stay on the mainland or come back to camp late?" I asked. "Like around two in the morning?"

Looking me square in the eye, Josh asked, "What's with the third degree?"

"I—well, I was up late Friday night and saw a boat heading this way. I just wondered if it might have been you."

"Probably." Kevin stretched and yawned. "We got back to camp around two." Kevin was shorter and stockier than his friend.

"Hey, what say we eat?" Josh ducked into the tent and opened a large cooler. "Kevin and I have been at the dig site all morning."

"You kids want a sandwich, something to drink?"

"We have stuff," Max said. "We could share. Mrs. T packed a bunch of fried chicken. Plus we've got chips and carrot sticks and lots of cookies."

"Cookies? Chicken?" Kevin all of a sudden didn't seem so tired. "I like the sound of that."

We sat on the blanket in the shade of some trees and set out the food. Mrs. Truesdale had packed enough for all of us. Kevin and Josh seemed happy to have company, and I don't think it was just for the food. They asked about us—what we liked, where we lived. Josh wanted to know about my bald head—I'd taken off my hat in the shade—so I told them about the leukemia.

"I have a cousin with leukemia," Kevin said. "She just turned twenty and has been in remission for like ten years."

"Jessie had a bone marrow transplant." Max pried the lid off the plastic container full of chocolate crinkle cookies and passed them around. "She should be good for another million miles."

I laughed. "You make me sound like a car."

Josh bit into his cookie and smiled. "Ah, heaven."

Max seemed pleased. "Good. I made them last night."

"I'm glad you kids came by," Josh said. "It's nice having company."

Kevin didn't seem quite as enthusiastic, but his mood was much better than it had been.

Cooper passed on the cookies. "You said you've been out here for a week?"

"More or less." Josh snatched another cookie.

"Are you the only ones on the island?"

Kevin raised an eyebrow. "As far as I know."

"So all the time you've been here you haven't had any other kids come by?"

Josh pulled off his hat and wiped the sweat off his forehead. "Should we have?"

"Naw." Cooper brushed some sand off the blanket. "I was just wondering."

"We haven't seen any indication that there's anybody on the island but us," Josh said. "You know it's a restricted area, don't you? In fact, you guys shouldn't even be here."

"Yeah, we know," I said as I picked up the napkins and stuffed them into a plastic bag.

"Kevin and I have special permits through the university. Professor Logan is supervising the dig."

"Where is your professor?" I asked.

"He had to go back to Seattle to take care of some business. He'll be back in two or three days." Josh grinned. "Hey, I get it. You're playing some kind of game and these other kids are hiding from you, right?"

"Not exactly," Cooper said, "but we are looking for someone.

We thought we'd row around the island just to make sure."

"Whatever." Josh turned serious. "You'd better hope your friends aren't here. Not only is it against the law; there's at least one cougar sharing the island with us."

"A cougar?" Ghost Island, like most of the others, was part of the national forest, but the island seemed too small for cougars. And I doubted a cougar could swim all the way from the mainland.

"Right—the forestry service isn't sure how he got out here. They're thinking maybe he was a pet and someone turned him loose. Or maybe he rode over on a log. Fortunately, there are plenty of deer and rabbits here for him to eat. One thing for sure—you kids don't want to go wandering around out here by yourself."

I put my hat back on. "We won't."

"What about you?" Max asked. "Aren't you afraid the cougar will attack while you're digging?"

"We have guns in case there's trouble." Kevin shrugged. "But I'm not worried. He's probably more scared of us than we are of him."

"Well, Kev, we should get back to work."

"That's what we're here for."

Josh drained his can of Coke. "Did you kids want to see what we've unearthed before you leave?"

"Sure." Max started to follow them.

Their finds weren't all that exciting, though they acted like they'd unearthed some national treasures. They had a table in their tent and on top of it lay several broken pieces of pottery, some arrowheads, and a lot of what looked like chunks of dirt. "Wow," Max said, "this is all you have from the whole week?"

Josh smiled down at her. "Well, we did find an intact necklace last week, but that's unusual. Archeology is a science, Max. It's painstaking and precise. We spend most of our time sifting through dirt. It's like digging a ditch with a spoon. Sometimes it takes us an hour to dig down an inch. Some people have come out here and found nothing at all."

I congratulated the guys and tried to hurry Max and Cooper along. It was already two, and we hadn't even begun to search for Enrique and his sisters. Josh walked down to the dock with us, carrying the picnic basket and blanket. Once he'd helped us into the boat, he released the rope and tossed it to Cooper. "Off you go. Come back and see us again." Josh waved. "And bring cookies."

"We will!" Max rocked the boat with her enthusiastic wave.

"What now?" Cooper asked when we'd gotten well away from the dock. "Want to keep looking here? You heard the guys. They haven't seen anyone."

"That doesn't mean anything," I said. "Ghost Island isn't all that big, but there are a lot of trees and about 600 acres. Besides, the fire we smelled didn't come from their fire pit."

"How do you know?"

"I looked. It was totally cold. There hasn't been a fire in it at all today."

"Which means someone else is here." Max frowned. "Let's go find them before the cougar does."

CHAPTER SEVEN

We rowed all the way around the island and still saw no sign that Enrique or anyone other than the archeologists had been there. It was getting late, and on the way back home we finished up the leftover snacks. Josh and Kevin had cleaned us out of chicken and cookies, but we still had a bag of chips and some carrots. Nibbling on a carrot, Max said, "I'll bet Enrique saw the archeologists' camp and went to another island."

"I hope so," Cooper said. "With that cougar on the island, they're in even more danger than we thought."

"Maybe he's not out here at all." I was supertired and getting grumpy. "Face it, guys—we really don't have a clue."

Cooper scowled and rowed a little harder. "What about the smoke you smelled?"

"It could have drifted over from the mainland."

"I'll bet anything he's out here on the lake somewhere. There are just too many places to hide."

"So what do we do?" I asked.

"We can check out some of the other islands." Cooper settled the oars across his lap and massaged his shoulders. "But we'll need a boat with a motor for sure."

I nodded. "We can probably use ours."

"Or Mrs. T's," Max added as she dug into the bag for some tortilla chips.

"Do you want me to start the motor now?" Max asked. "Or I could row for a while?"

"I'm okay. We're almost to Jessie's dock." He dipped the oars into the water again. "Maybe we should go out to Bear Island. That's where your boat drifted, Jessie, and where I broke my arm. I had a cool camp there, and I told Enrique about it. He said we should go there sometime. It's a lot farther than Ghost Island, but . . ."

"He'd never be able to row that far," Max interrupted.

"You're probably right," Cooper said, then mumbled something about Enrique having a motorboat.

"That doesn't make sense unless he stole it," I said, then right away wished I hadn't.

"Maybe he had to, okay?" Cooper snarled at me. He looked down and shook his head. "I'm sorry, Jess. I didn't mean to yell."

"It's okay. If Enrique stole anything, it would be to protect his sisters." I brushed away the tears gathering in my eyes. No one said anything as we approached the dock.

Cooper had no sooner gotten out of the boat to tie up than my dad came running down the sloping yard. "It's about time you kids showed up. I was getting ready to call out a search party."

"It's not that late," I said, looking down at my watch. Six thirty actually, which was late for me since I usually tire out by two and need a nap.

Dad's concerned gaze slid over my face. "Did you have fun?"

"We did, sir," Cooper answered. "Did you know there were archeologists out on Ghost Island?"

"Actually, I did. There was an article in the paper about a week ago. You kids weren't out there bothering them, were you?"

"No." I took Dad's hand as he helped me out of the boat. "Kevin and Josh invited us to eat lunch with them, and they showed us the artifacts they'd found."

"It was pretty cool, Mr. Miller," Max said. "I've never seen a dig before."

"Kevin and Josh, huh? Sounds like you made a couple of new friends."

"Yeah. They were cool." Max grinned. "College students from the University of Washington."

Dad nodded. "Did you meet their professor?"

I shook my head. "They were alone. Professor Logan went into Seattle. He'll be back in a few days."

"It sounds like you had an interesting day." Dad snatched up the picnic basket and walked up to the house with us. "Dinner's about ready. You kids want to join us?"

Both Max and Cooper said they had to call home.

"Dad's not home, so I left a message." Cooper pocketed his cell phone. "He won't mind."

Max used the kitchen phone to call Amelia. "Oh, right," she

said into the phone. "I forgot. I'll be home in half an hour." She hung up and waved at us as she headed out the back door.

"Max!" I yelled after her. "What's going on?"

"I gotta get home." She paused. "I promised Mrs. T that I'd help her make lavender sachets and wrap scones. I was supposed to be home by four."

"Is she mad at you?"

"Mrs. T?" Max seemed surprised by the question. "Nope. She's cool. I just don't like to disappoint her, that's all."

"Do you want me to help? We could get a lot more done."

"Sure. If it's okay with your mom and dad."

Mom set the tossed salad on the table. "I'd rather you didn't, Jessie. You need to rest. In fact, I want you to stay home for a couple of days. You have a doctor's appointment tomorrow and . . ."

I couldn't believe what I was hearing. I felt like crying and throwing a fit, but I didn't want to embarrass my friends. I also didn't want to argue with Mom and Dad in front of Max and Cooper.

"I'll call you later, Jess." Max waved as she went out the patio door.

"Wait up, Max." Cooper mumbled something about needing to go back with Max to Lakeside Farm so he could pick up his bike.

I went out and sat on the steps until they were gone, then stumbled back inside. Instead of sitting down at the table with my family, I went up to my room and fell on my bed. I didn't know whether to whine, yell, or cry. How could Mom do this to me?

Part of me understood. I hadn't been out of the hospital all that long, and they were probably worried that I would get sick again. I couldn't blame them; I was a little worried about that myself. I'd been out almost all day—eight hours. I was tired, but I didn't feel sick—not like I used to before the bone marrow transplant. I probably should rest for a day or two, but how in the world was I supposed to help Max and Cooper find Enrique?

"Jessie?" Mom came in. The mattress shifted as she sat down and rubbed my back. "Are you feeling okay?"

"I *feel* fine. I'm not sick, and I shouldn't have to stay home. I didn't do anything wrong."

"I know. It's just that you don't seem to be using much common sense. You're supposed to take it easy, not run yourself ragged."

I turned over so I could look at her. The worry on her face kept me from getting mad. "I wasn't running. I was sitting in a boat most of the time. Max and Cooper rowed the whole time."

"I understand that. But Jessie, you're still not 100 percent. You're pushing yourself harder than you should, and that worries me."

"But, Mom, I feel fine." That wasn't exactly true, so I wasn't surprised when she raised an eyebrow at me.

"No, you don't. You're exhausted. You have dark shadows under your eyes."

"But I don't feel sick. Not like before the transplant."

"Jessie." Mom looked like she was about to cry. I hated that look. It made me feel guilty, even when I didn't deserve to feel that way.

"Okay." I turned away from her. "I'll stay home tomorrow."

"Yes, you will. We'll go see Dr. Caldwell. I'm all for you being able to do things with your friends. Just promise me you'll listen to her advice about taking care of yourself." She rubbed my shoulder and stood up. "How about coming down to eat?"

"I guess." I sighed and scooted off the bed, telling her I needed to use the bathroom first. Looking at my face in the mirror turned out to be a huge mistake. I could see why Mom was worried. What I saw worried me too. I did have shadows, and I looked almost as bad as I did last time I got sick. I closed my eyes, not wanting to think about what this might mean. Had the bone marrow transplant failed? *Oh, God, please don't let me get sick again. Please.*

CHAPTER EIGHT

I felt better the next morning and a lot less worried. I'd gone to bed around eight after taking a long bath. Although I wouldn't be sure until I saw my doctor, I felt certain my weariness was from being overtired and not from the leukemia.

Max called while I was getting dressed. Mom brought the phone up to my room.

"Hey, Jess." Max sounded worried. "You doing okay?"

"Sure, but I can't go with you and Cooper to look for Enrique today."

"I figured that much. We're not going today anyway. I need to help Mrs. T, and Coop says he should stay home and work on the yard. His dad's been bugging him."

I bit my lip as a lump caught in my throat. I knew if they really wanted to go out on the lake they could. "Thanks, Max. You're a true friend."

"Sure, but what's that got to do with anything? Listen, your mom said you had a doctor's appointment today. Good luck with that. Call me and tell me what your doctor says."

"I will."

Since I'd gotten up so late, the morning whizzed by, and before I knew it, Mom was calling me from downstairs. "We need to leave in a couple minutes, Jessie. Are you ready?"

"Be right down." I closed down my computer. Maybe I couldn't actually go out to search for Enrique, but I could do some research. I had found quite a few situations like Enrique's. One family in Walla Walla, which is in the southeast part of our state, was about to be deported back to England. They'd moved to the U.S. about 16 years ago, but had never gotten their U.S. citizenship. They had two girls, teenagers, who had not been born in the U.S., but they didn't know it. A lot of people in the town were supporting the family, trying to keep them from having to leave. But the authorities weren't listening.

I'd read both sides of the story and understood how important it was for the immigration authorities to enforce the law. But I felt sad for the family—especially the girls who were still in high school. How awful to have to leave your friends and school to go to another country.

England might not be so bad, I thought, but I wasn't so sure about Mexico. Poor Enrique. How long could he and his sisters stay hidden? What were they doing for food?

"Jessie!" Mom's not-too-patient voice stopped my worries and sent me rushing down the stairs.

I hoped Dr. Caldwell would tell my mother to stop being so worried and to let me hang out with my friends. I wanted to go out with Max and Cooper tomorrow for sure. I had a bad feeling about Enrique and the girls.

The doctor's visit went a lot faster than I thought it would. They sent me to the lab to get my blood drawn, and then we waited for the results. Sam had come along, so we worked on a puzzle. I didn't get really nervous until the nurse took me back to the exam room by myself.

I got up on the table and watched the nurse take my blood pressure and check my temperature and pulse. She didn't flinch or anything, so I guessed everything was normal. When she left, I got off the table and looked through the ancient magazines in the rack. *Natural Health* had an article on powering up your immune system. I started reading it and put it back when the door opened. I had wanted to go in by myself, but now I was wishing Mom and Sam had come in too. I could imagine the doctor telling me I had to go back into the hospital. That I had been too active and my body was rejecting the bone marrow.

Dr. Caldwell smiled when she came into the room. "Hi, Jessie."

"Hi." I swallowed hard. *She's smiling. How bad can it be?*

"How are you feeling?" She placed her hands under my ears and along my chin to feel my glands.

"Tired, I guess, but I'm doing okay."

"Your mother tells me you've been overdoing it."

I frowned. "She worries too much."

Dr. Caldwell nodded. "That's what mothers are supposed to do." She checked my ears and throat and listened to my heart and lungs. When she finished the exam she slipped the stethoscope back around her neck. "Well, Jessie . . ."

"So, am I going to die?"

"I don't think we need to worry about that just yet. Your blood work looks good. No surprises."

I closed my eyes and heaved a huge sigh. "That means I can hang with my friends, right? You can tell Mom not to worry?"

Her smile slipped away. "We're not out of the woods yet, Jessie. Your mother is right to be concerned. She said you were out on the water and picnicking for over eight hours yesterday."

"Most of the time I was just sitting in the boat. I don't want to just stay home."

"You can be as active as you feel like being. Remember the deal we made when you first started back to public school?"

"Like I could forget." I rolled my eyes and recited the list. "Listen to my body and my parents. Don't push too hard. Stop when I feel myself getting tired. Eat well-balanced meals; take my medications."

Dr. Caldwell chuckled. "I'll tell your mom to go easy on you. But, Jessie, more freedom comes with a price. You need to be responsible for your own care. Don't do things that are going to set you back. If you do that you force others, like myself and your parents, to make decisions for you."

I nodded that I understood. And I did. It's just that being friends with normal kids like Max and Cooper makes it hard to stick to the rules.

We went back out to the waiting room, where Dr. Caldwell talked to my mother, going over the things we'd covered. On the way home I leaned back and closed my eyes, mostly so Mom wouldn't lecture me and go over the same stuff again. When we got home, I went upstairs.

I got lost in my favorite mystery series and stayed there until dinner. After that I helped with dishes and then settled on the couch and watched the news with Dad. The newscasters mentioned that the Sanchez children were still missing and then went right into a report about the string of robberies. "Police are not making the connection between the missing children and the robberies as yet, but will be carefully examining the evidence."

I leaned forward. "Did they just say what I thought they said? They think Enrique is involved in the robberies?"

Dad pushed the mute button when a commercial came on. "The robberies started shortly before Enrique and his sisters disappeared. The police have to look at every angle."

"That's just not right. Enrique wouldn't do anything like that."

Dad rubbed my shoulder. "I can appreciate your wanting to stand up for him, Jessie, but he had to be desperate to run away."

I couldn't stand to watch any more news, so I went back upstairs to read.

It was getting dark outside when Mom poked her head in my room. "Are you too tired to go with me to the store, Jessie?"

"Which one?" I was hoping for the mall in Lakeside, but realized it was too late for that.

"I need to pick up some groceries at Hansen's. Thought you might like to get out for a while. Your dad is watching a Mariners game, and he wants ice cream."

"Sure." I got my shoes on and hurried after her. "I can go. Is Sam coming?"

She laughed. "Of course."

A few minutes later we pulled into Hansen's parking lot. "It won't take me too long. Maybe you could watch Sam."

"Can I ride the bouncing horse and the car?" Sam asked, running ahead.

"Sure." When we got inside, Mom handed me some change. "That will give him three rides. I should be done by then."

Sam climbed up on the horse, and I plugged two quarters into it. For the next few minutes Sam pretended to be a rodeo rider. Then a race car driver. At about the middle of Sam's third ride, Cooper came in and stopped to talk. "How'd your doctor's appointment go?" he asked.

"Good." I grinned up at him. I swear, every time I see him he's grown another inch.

"Max and I are going out on the lake again tomorrow. Do you think you can come?"

"Definitely. Did you see the news?"

"Yeah, and I can't believe they're . . ."

"I need more quarters." Sam yanked at my arm.

Annoyed at him for interrupting, I said, "You used all Mom gave me."

"I want to ride some more."

"Sorry, Sam, I can't help you. Just wait. Mom will be done soon." I turned my attention back to Cooper. "What time are you going out?"

"Early. Around eight. If it's okay, I'll come to your place and Max will pick us up in the boat."

"I'll have to check with my parents, but it should work."

"Are you ready to go, Jessie?" Mom pushed the cart toward us. "Hi, Cooper."

Cooper grinned. "Hi, Mrs. Miller. Jessie and I were talking about her, Max, and me going out on the lake again tomorrow. Are you okay with that?"

"Um . . ." She glanced at me, and I could tell she was struggling between wanting to protect me and letting me go. She cleared her throat. "That will work."

I smiled and gave her a hug. "Thanks, Mom."

She hugged me back. "We should go." Glancing over at the rides, she asked, "Where's Sam?"

My happiness dropped into my shoes as my heart flipped over. "He was right here a second ago. He wanted more money for the rides. He must have gone to find you."

"Jessie . . ." Mom pinched her lips together, probably to keep from getting mad at me in front of Cooper. "All right. We'll just have to look for him."

"I'll help," Cooper offered.

Mom nodded. "Jessie, take the bakery and deli area; Cooper,

check the fruit department. I'll do the aisles."

We took off to our appointed sections and several minutes later came back to the checkstand area. None of us had found him. "All right, you two look again. I'll talk to the manager and see if he can page Sam."

I heard the page over the PA system and thought Sam would get a kick out of hearing his name. Mom was having him go to the ice-cream section. That should do it. I headed that way. Cooper showed up, and Mom, but no Sam. I was really getting scared. I'd seen too many newscasts about kids being kidnapped. "I'm sorry, Mom." Tears clouded my vision. "I should have been watching him better."

Mom's arms came around me. "It's not your fault, honey. Sam wasn't listening."

By now we'd managed to attract a lot of attention. The store security officer introduced himself and told us he'd called the police. They'd check through the store again and branch out into the surrounding area. He told us to stay where we were in case Sam heard the pages.

I wiped my eyes with the backs of my hands. I tried to think about what I would do if I were in Sam's place. He probably wasn't even scared yet, or missing us. Why hadn't he heard the page? "Mom, I have an idea. He's not in the store. Maybe he's in the car."

"Good thinking. It's locked, but he could be waiting beside it."

I hurried out to the parking lot, but saw no sign of Sam near the car or anywhere else. The police car was just pulling into the parking lot when I reached the side of the store. "Sam," I called. No one answered.

I thought I heard a rustling sound and hurried back along the side of the store. Darkness closed in on me. The streetlight didn't reach back here, and I wondered why there was no light in back of the store. Still, I could make out the form of an open Dumpster. I jumped back as a dark figure brushed by me, ducked into the bushes, and headed for the lake. I started to follow when I heard footsteps behind me. A heavy hand came down on my shoulder.

"Hold it right there."

CHAPTER NINE

I probably should have said something to the police officer about the person I'd seen, but for several seconds I was too scared to move. I couldn't have talked if I'd tried. By the time I realized who had come up behind me and practically dragged me back into the store, I realized something else too. The guy who'd run into the bushes might have been Enrique. It made sense. Enrique was probably looking for food. Smart thinking. Grocery stores throw out a lot of food. I've heard about charity groups getting tons of perishable foods that were about to get thrown out, but they were still perfectly good to eat.

"Did you find my brother?" I asked the officer.

He said he didn't know. He led me back to where Mom was waiting. "He wasn't in the parking lot," I told her. "I was checking around the side and back when this officer caught me."

"You shouldn't have been out there alone," the officer said. "If you'll excuse me, I need to check in." He said something into his radio mike and walked away.

"I'm really getting worried." Mom pulled me into a hug. "I can't imagine where he could have gone."

"You know Sam. Maybe he saw somebody he knows or something. They'll find him." *They have to.* I couldn't let myself even think that someone had taken him. I thought about the Dumpster and the person I'd seen running away. Sam knew Enrique and went to school with Maela Sanchez, Enrique's youngest sister. Had the girls been with Enrique? Could Sam have seen them and maybe gone with them?

"Maybe he's out in back of the store," I said, "by the loading dock."

"I'm sure someone from the store has looked there already," Mom said.

"Probably, but I think I'll look again."

I met Cooper in front of the meat department. "I need to talk to you." I looked around and pointed toward the back entrance of the store. "Let's check around the loading dock."

On the way I told him about the person I'd seen running away. "It was dark, but I got to thinking it might be Enrique. He might have been looking for food."

"You didn't tell the police . . ."

"Not yet." It upset me that he'd think I would.

"Well, don't." Cooper's long stride put me about ten feet behind him. I had to run to catch up. "I'm worried that Sam saw him or his sisters. He might have followed them."

Cooper turned and I almost ran into him. "Stay here. I can go faster alone."

As much as I hated being left behind, he was right. He could go a lot faster without me. While I waited for him, I poked around the cartons and boxes looking for Sam, but had no luck. I finally headed back to the front of the store. The police were looking around the neighborhood by now. The manager was still trying to console my mother.

"I think we'd better call your father." Mom pulled the cell phone out of her purse and started punching buttons.

"Honey, Jessie," Dad said as he came up behind us. "The police called me. What's going on?"

"Dan." Mom closed the phone and stepped into his arms for a hug. Dad reached for me too.

"We need to go home in case Sam goes there," Dad said. "The police said they'd cover the store in case he shows up here. They're already canvassing the area between here and home."

Mom held up one of the grocery bags. "Oh, no. The ice cream is all melted." Mom seemed to be having a meltdown too.

"Don't worry about it." The store manager took the bag and tossed it into the garbage. "I'll get you a fresh carton, Mrs. Miller."

"Thank you." Mom couldn't seem to stop crying now, and it had nothing to do with the ice cream. Dad took her out to the van while I waited for the manager. Not that any of us would be hungry for ice cream or anything else.

Cooper came back into the store. His expression told me he hadn't found Sam. I told him what Dad had said.

"That's a good idea. I'll help the cops look for him for a while. Call me on my cell if you hear anything."

"I will. Thank you."

He nodded and then took off. The manager had brought the ice cream by then, so I hurried out to the van. "What about the car?" I asked as I climbed into the backseat.

"We can pick it up tomorrow," Dad said. "I don't think it's a good idea for your mom to drive right now."

I didn't either. She reached for another tissue and blew her nose.

When we got home, the lights were on, just like Dad had left them. Everything seemed normal, but it wasn't.

I wondered if it ever would be again. Where could Sam have gone? Had someone from the store taken him? Had he seen Enrique and followed him? Sam knew our town nearly as well as I did. He'd walked home from school with me several times. So where was he?

I went out the patio door and down to our dock. Some of the yard lights were on, causing trees to cast eerie shadows across the lawns. The lake looked cold and dark. I shivered, glad for my sweatshirt. Noticing the tree fort, I wandered over to it. Sam spent a lot of time here playing with the twins. I climbed up the ladder and ducked inside. Thanks to the yard light, I could make out the location of the beanbag chairs and the low table. I settled into one of the bags by the window and stared out at the lake. Sam could be a pest, but I loved the little guy.

I don't think I'd ever felt so helpless. I couldn't stand not doing anything, but what could I do?

Pretty soon I felt myself nodding off, so I left the tree house and went back inside. I didn't want to go to sleep, but Mom told me I should. We compromised by me snuggling on the couch next to her.

The next thing I knew it was daylight. Mom and Dad were sitting at the table with coffee cups in their hands. I knew without asking that Sam hadn't been found—and that neither of them had slept. I heated water for hot chocolate and sat down at the table. "Have you heard anything?" I asked.

"They brought in dogs last night." Dad took a sip of coffee. "They picked up the trail at the grocery store and . . ." Dad set the coffee down and pinched the bridge of his nose. Mom laid a hand on his arm. She seemed more calm this morning.

"What?" I didn't want to upset them more, but I had to know.

"Sam's trail ended at the lake."

I pulled up my knees and hugged them. The beeper on the microwave went off, but I didn't move. There was no way Sam would just walk into the lake. Someone had had a boat down there, and I felt certain that someone was Enrique. If Sam went with him, he went willingly. That kid had a scream that could be heard two states away. Unless someone had gagged him.

"It's crazy." Dad sucked in a deep breath and reached for his cup again. "The authorities are suggesting that he may have stumbled across someone doing something illegal and they took him to keep him from talking. I don't know what to think. They're searching the lake this morning. I'm heading out in a few minutes."

"Dad . . ." I was about to tell him about Enrique when I caught a movement out of the corner of my eye. I stared at the stairs, my mouth hanging open. "It's him."

"Sam!" Mom and Dad yelled at once. They moved so fast, I swear their chairs were still wobbling when they reached the stairs. Dad grabbed Sam and lifted him up into his arms. Mom wrapped her arms around both of them. Totally confused, I pushed myself into the mix.

"Where have you been?" I asked when things settled down.

"That's a very good question, Sam." Dad hunkered down in front of Sam and Mom, who were now sitting on the steps.

"Sleepin'." Sam yawned. "What's going on?"

Mom sobbed and hugged him again.

"We've been looking all over for you." I couldn't decide whether to be mad or really, really glad. Both, I guess. "One minute you're in the store and the next, you disappeared."

He giggled. "I didn't disappear. You're funny."

"It's not funny, Son." Dad placed his hands on his knees and stood up. "What happened out there? What were you doing down at the lake?"

Sam raised his eyebrows as if the news had surprised him. He cocked his head and shrugged his shoulders.

"Are you saying you don't remember?" Dad frowned, and I could tell he didn't believe him. Sam put his thumb in his mouth, closed his eyes, and buried his face against Mom's chest.

"Not now." She looked up at Dad and me and wrapped her arms tighter around Sam. "Come on, sleepyhead," she said. "How about I fix you some strawberry pancakes with whipped cream?"

He lifted his head and nodded. She planted a kiss on his forehead. "You can tell us all about your adventure later." Dad picked him up and carried him to the kitchen table while Mom went ahead. Sam turned around and looked straight at me. I'm not sure how I knew, but I did. I had no doubt that Sam remembered everything about the night before, and he had no intention of telling Mom or Dad. He would tell me though. I'd make sure of that.

CHAPTER TEN

As promised, Max came rowing up to our dock at 8:30. Now that Sam was home and safe, I asked my parents if I could go out on the lake with Max and Cooper. They said yes right away. I think they were too tired to argue.

"I heard you found Sam," Max yelled from the dock.

"How did you find out?"

"Cooper."

I nodded. I had called Cooper right after Sam showed up.

I went down to meet her. "He was in his room, sleeping. I don't know for how long, but he must have come home last night while Dad was at the store picking us up."

"What did he do, walk home?"

"More like he got somebody to take him in their boat." I explained about the dogs and how his scent had vanished at the lake behind the store. "I think it was Enrique." Then I told her about seeing someone run past me into the bushes. "It's still a mystery, but I bet Sam will tell me. At least I hope so. He sure isn't talking to Mom and Dad."

"Maybe he's too scared to talk," Max suggested.

I shook my head. "That's what he wants our parents to believe. Sam isn't scared, which is why I'm sure it was someone he knows."

"I don't get it." Max finished tying up the boat and brushed her hands off on her baggy pants. "Why would Enrique take Sam with him and then drop him off at home?"

I shrugged. "I don't know. If the guy I saw was Enrique, he was trying to get away fast. I didn't see Sam then, but I'm hoping Sam can tell us. Let's invite him to go for a boat ride with us. That way we can get him alone."

"Good thinking." She looked past me and grinned. "Hey, Coop, it's about time you got here."

I twisted around in time to see Cooper rest his bike against the side of the house and start jogging toward us. "Sorry about that." Looking at me he said, "What's the deal with Sam? Did you say he wasn't missing after all?"

"Oh, he was missing all right." I quickly filled him in and then went inside to get Sam.

It took me ten minutes to convince Mom to let Sam come on a boat ride with us. She finally gave in when Dad took her aside. They talked in low tones, and I couldn't hear much except that Dad thought it might help Sam relax. Mom had that I-know-when-I'm-beat look when she came back to where Sam and I were standing. "All right. You know the rules. Life jacket on at all times, sunscreen, water . . ."

"I know, Mom." To Sam I said, "Go get dressed—hurry." I

thought about adding *before they change their minds* but decided that wouldn't be the best move right now. Instead I grabbed some bottled water out of the fridge and told Mom and Dad we were just going to take him for a short ride. "We'll have him back in an hour."

Mom nodded. "I'm going to call Dr. Campbell and make an appointment for this afternoon. He seems to be okay, but . . . I'm concerned that he won't talk about what happened."

"That's a good idea." I didn't know what else to say. I hated seeing Mom so worried, and I thought I should have told her about my suspicions right then and there, but I didn't know for sure. Better to wait and hear what Sam had to say. That is, if he'd say anything at all.

"Where to?" Cooper asked once we'd pushed away from the dock.

I pointed toward town. Cooper and Max seemed to know right away what I was thinking. My plan was to time the trip from my house to the dock behind Hansen's Grocery.

"You okay, Sam?" Max asked.

He nodded but didn't say anything.

"Everybody was worried about you."

"I know. Mom told me. Are you in trouble cause of me, Jessie?"

The sad look in his eyes almost made me cry. "Not really. Mom was more mad at you than at me."

"Good."

Cooper grunted. "So, Sam, where did you go? I mean, I've

never seen anybody disappear that fast. It's almost like you were planning to escape the whole time."

Sam jerked his head up. "I didn't. I was just . . ." His big blue eyes filled with tears. "I can't tell."

"It's okay, buddy." I reached forward and pulled him back against me.

"Why are we here?" Sam twisted around to face me.

"I wanted to see how long it took. I know what happened last night." We had made it to the dock in fifteen minutes.

"You do?" He scowled at me then and said, "No, you don't. You're trying to trick me."

"I'm not. Let me tell you what I think happened."

Sam folded his skinny arms and pinched his lips together.

"After you left me, you went to look for Mom. I'm not sure why you went to the loading dock—maybe you were curious. You saw somebody back there, didn't you? Someone you know. Was it Enrique? Or one of his sisters? He was digging through the Dumpster looking for food."

The size of Sam's eyes and the surprise registered there told me I was on the right track. "I saw Enrique run past me," I said, "but I didn't see you. How did you get to the boat?"

He didn't answer my question at first. He seemed more concerned that I'd guessed what had happened. "He was afraid I'd tell on him."

Anger toward Enrique rose like the acid in my stomach. He may have been trying to protect his sisters, but he had no business involving my little brother. "What did he do?"

"He just told me to be quiet so the police wouldn't hurt us. He picked me up and carried me to the boat, and then we rowed away." Sam must have sensed my anger because he said, "It's okay, Jessie. He din't hurt me. He just had to get us away from there. He dropped me off at home and said he was sorry if he scared me. Enrique said not to tell anybody he was there. If the police find him or his sisters, they would make them go far away to Mexico. Maela is my friend. I don't want the police to take her."

Sam brushed tears from his cheeks with his arm.

"Why didn't you let us know you were home?" My anger diminished as I tried to see the situation from Enrique's viewpoint.

"Nobody was home, so I went to bed. I didn't want to talk to Mom and Dad cause they mighta made me tell."

I gave him a squeeze. I could understand why Enrique took Sam. He must have felt trapped, but asking a little kid to keep secrets like that isn't fair.

"You aren't going to tell anybody, are you?" Sam asked.

"No," Cooper said. "We're trying to find Enrique so we can help them. Did Enrique tell you where they were staying?"

Sam shook his head. "He just dropped me off and went back out on the lake."

"Which way did he go?" Max asked.

"That way." Sam pointed up the lake—toward Ghost Island. Cooper, Max, and I looked at each other, sending a silent message. We'd have to go back and look again.

CHAPTER ELEVEN

When we got back to my house, we dropped Sam off. I told Max and Cooper to wait while I went up to talk to my parents about Sam. I didn't want to tell them about Enrique, but I didn't think we had a choice. It wasn't fair to put a burden like that on Sam. I couldn't lie to them, and I didn't want Sam to either.

On the way up to the house, I reminded Sam about good secrets and bad secrets. "Good secrets are . . . like birthday surprises or Christmas presents or doing something nice for someone. Bad secrets are like when people get hurt."

"But if you tell Mom and Dad, they might tell the police, and they'll take Enrique and Callista and Maela away."

"Maybe not. We don't know where they are." When we got to the deck, I pulled Sam down on the step beside me. "Enrique's secret isn't so bad. The bad part is that if we don't tell Mom and Dad what really happened to you, they'll be worried. They'll think something really bad happened. And that would hurt them. Do you understand?"

"I guess so."

I took his hand and stood up. Then, taking a deep breath, I led him inside.

Our parents took the news a lot better than I thought they would. They even seemed understanding when I asked them to please not tell the police it was Enrique.

Dad hugged me. "You made the right decision in telling us about Enrique, Princess. As far as telling the police, all I can promise you is that we'll pray about it and consider all the options. I'm sure Enrique thinks he's doing the right thing, but he may be putting his sisters in danger."

"But, Dad." I stepped out of his hug. "We can't let the immigration people send them to Mexico."

"There are worse things. As I understand it, they have family there. Before I tell the police anything about Enrique, I'll talk to his aunt. There are right and wrong ways to handle situations like this, Jessie. I know that you, Cooper, and Max are looking for Enrique. I hope you find him. And if you do, convince him to come back to his aunt's place."

"I'll think about it."

I hurried back to the boat dock where Max and Cooper were laughing about something. They stopped when my feet hit the dock. "Hey, Jess," Max said. "We were just about to leave without you."

They must have read the guilty look on my face because Max tugged on Cooper's arm. "Uh-oh. You told your parents, didn't you?"

I swallowed the lump in my throat and ducked my head. I knew that by telling Mom and Dad I'd taken a chance that my friends might get mad at me. "I had to. It wasn't right to have them worry like that."

To Cooper, Max said, "This is what we get for having an honest friend. What do you think, Coop? Should we take her with us?"

Cooper winked at me to let me know they were teasing. "Depends on how fast she can get into the boat."

I released the breath I'd been holding and even smiled a little as I climbed into Max's canoe with them. Cooper handed me a life jacket. I put it on and then adjusted my scarf. "You guys knew I'd tell all along, didn't you?"

Max chuckled. "Yeah, well, I'm thinking you pretty much had to."

"So you're not mad at me?"

"I just have one question." Cooper looked right in my eyes. "If we find Enrique, are you going to turn him in?"

I bit my lower lip and looked away for a second. Then I looked back up at him and said, "I don't know. I guess it depends on whether or not it's the right thing to do."

"I guess we can live with that."

We hadn't gotten very far from shore when Cooper leaned to the side. I thought he was going to tip us over. "Hey, did you see that?"

"What?" I gripped the sides of the canoe and followed his gaze.

“There’s something floating in the water. Something red.”

“I see it,” Max yelled.

I saw a flash of red about halfway between us and Ghost Island that disappeared and then popped back up again, probably rising and falling with the wave action.

“Did you bring your binoculars?” Max asked.

I dug them out of my bag and took off the lens covers. When I held them up to my eyes, all I could see was water moving up and down. “Ugh. It’s making me seasick.” I handed them to Max, who didn’t seem to have any trouble at all. “Can you tell what it is?” I asked.

“Looks like one of those swim toys.”

Cooper rowed for fifteen minutes before we came up alongside it. Max had been right. It was a toy—one of those floaty rings for little kids. Max scooped it up and examined it.

“Some kid probably threw it off a boat.” Cooper looked disappointed.

“Maybe Maela lost it,” Max said. “Look, it has the initials MS written on it. I think we should take it with us to show Leah.”

“I guess it couldn’t hurt.” Cooper pulled up the oar and grimaced.

“What’s wrong, Cooper?” I asked.

“Max, take over the rowing for me, okay?”

“Sure.” Max took the oar and started rowing toward the island.

I didn’t think Cooper was going to answer me. He had his eyes closed and was rubbing the arm he'd broken. I knew it must be hurting, but his expression told me there was more going on.

"It's my dad." Cooper shifted his gaze from Max to me. "I tried to talk to him about Enrique last night. He told me not to waste my time worrying about them. He wants the authorities to round up all the illegals and ship them back to Mexico—even Enrique and his sisters. I can't believe he could be so mean."

"Bummer," Max said. "Mrs. T says there should be special circumstances for the children—especially in a case like this where their aunt was born here."

"Maybe we should stop looking for them," Cooper said. "I mean, what if we do find them? What are we going to do? If we help them we might lead the cops right to them."

I didn't know what to say. "I want to find them—make sure they're okay. If they're on Ghost Island, we need to warn them about the cougar."

"We know Enrique is all right. At least he was last night."

"So, what are you saying, Coop? You really want to give up?" Max kept rowing toward the island.

"Not exactly. But trying to find them is like trying to find a guppy in the ocean."

I fingered the letters on the red toy. "We have a clue. There's a chance this floaty belongs to Maela. Think about it. If we follow the current up-lake from here, I bet it'll go right to Ghost Island."

Cooper studied the water. "Okay. Let's take the float toy to Mrs. Estrada and see if it's Maela's. If it is, we can look at the current charts. Maybe we can get an idea of where on the island it went into the water. It's a long shot and I'm still wondering if Enrique and his sisters might be better off without our help."

Max and I looked at each other. From the determined look on her face, I could tell that, like me, she wasn't going to give up even if Cooper did. I figured Enrique could take care of himself, but the girls were only five and nine years old. In order to get supplies, Enrique had to leave them alone. And if they were on Ghost Island, they'd be sharing it with a cougar and who knew what else.

We had to wait until four o'clock to talk to Leah. The minute she saw the swim toy, she started crying. Leah hugged the plastic ring to her chest and began rocking.

She thinks Maela is dead. The thought nearly doubled me over. For the first time I realized that Maela might have drowned. Why else would her swim toy be floating on the lake?

CHAPTER TWELVE

The thought that one or both of the girls might have drowned took my breath away. What if they had tried to swim to the island when they first ran away? Even with float toys, they wouldn't make it. The water warmed up a little in the summer, but not nearly enough. If they were in the deep water too long they'd get hypothermia.

"Please don't cry, Mrs. Estrada. If anything bad had happened to Callista or Maela, Enrique would have come back, wouldn't he?" I thought about what had happened the night before and added, "He had a boat."

Max nodded. "I'll bet Maela was playing in the water and dropped her swim toy and it drifted out too far."

I glanced over at Cooper, then at Max, and then sat down next to Leah and told her about seeing Enrique at the store.

"You saw him? You talked to him?"

"My brother did. Enrique told Sam not to tell anyone that he'd seen him. He had to protect his sisters. That means they're okay."

She sniffled and blew her nose. "Thank you for telling me this. I will keep hoping you are right."

"My parents were going to call and tell you about last night," I said.

"Yes. They left a message, and I have not called them back. I just came home from work. I have been so worried. Now I know the children have food and they are safe."

I wasn't so sure about the safe part, but didn't say so.

"You have no idea where they are?" Leah asked.

"Not yet," Cooper said. "But we'll keep looking."

She set the floaty aside. "I can't believe this is happening. It's all so confusing. I know the authorities think Carlos is illegal, but I don't believe that."

"What do you mean?" I asked.

She sighed. "Carlos didn't tell me much about his immigrant status, but I was sure he had a green card when he came here. When he was killed, I tried to tell the police that he wasn't illegal, but they couldn't find his papers. Or his green card."

"That doesn't make sense. Can't they just look him up?"

Leah shook her head. "Carlos Sanchez is a common name. Without papers, it could take weeks to find him in the system. They don't believe me, and I can't prove anything. Carlos didn't talk to me about these things. I honestly don't know if he was legal or not. His status doesn't really matter now anyway. What matters is that we find the children."

When we left Leah's place, it was well past noon. We decided we'd wait until tomorrow to go back out in the boat. In the meantime, Cooper would study the weather reports and marine charts of Chenoa Lake and try to determine where the toy might have been when it went into the water. I was still guessing Ghost Island.

The next day came, and unfortunately the adults in our lives had plans for us that did not include letting us go out on the lake. Cooper had called the night before around nine. "You were right, Jessie," he'd said. "According to my calculations, Maela's swim toy floated from Ghost Island. The problem is I can't go out tomorrow. Dad's taking me into town to buy a laptop for school. There's a big sale at Best Buy."

When I called Max, she said she should stay and help out on the farm. I supposed it was just as well because I had to take care of Sam while Mom and Dad went into Seattle. Seattle was two hours away, which took most of the day. In payment for taking care of my brother, they gave me permission to stay overnight with Max out at Lakeside Farm.

Amelia invited me for dinner, so Max came by with her canoe to pick me up as soon as Mom and Dad came home. I already had my stuff packed and was ready to go.

After dinner, we worked on sachets, and Amelia taught us how to make lavender wands while she baked cookies and scones. I could see why Max didn't mind staying home to help out. Doing the crafts was a lot of fun. Amelia had a lot of stories to tell about growing up on the farm. We started getting ready for bed around ten, and Amelia put on the news.

Max and I were making plans to go out on the lake the next morning and take a picnic lunch again. "I want to stop by and see Josh and Kevin."

I giggled at her expression. She so had a crush on Josh.

"Oh, dear." Amelia's cry caught our attention. "Girls, you're going to want to see this."

"What's wrong?" It didn't take me long to get the gist of what Amelia was talking about. The video showed Enrique being put into a police car while the newscaster told viewers that the search for the missing boy was over, but that the little girls had still not been found. The police had caught Enrique taking food from the Dumpster at the Quickie Mart in Chenoa Lake. They also said he'd stolen a rowboat from a resident near the lake.

"Immigration authorities have been seeking to deport the Sanchez children," the newscaster said, "but tonight, there's a new twist to the story. Police say Enrique Sanchez is a person of interest in the recent robberies in Chenoa Lake, Lakeside, and Hidden Springs. Over a dozen lakefront properties have been burglarized in the past two weeks."

"Enrique isn't the thief." Max pushed out of the chair and paced. "How can they think he did it?"

"The police generally don't arrest someone without evidence," Amelia said. "And the news anchor did say he was a person of interest, not that he was the burglar. On the other hand, he did steal that boat."

"His aunt told us they were questioning her too," I said. "I can understand why the police would question the homemakers. It makes sense to check out everyone who had keys to those houses. I suppose it's logical for the police to question Enrique since his aunt . . ."

"Whose side are you on, Jess?" Max gave me a dirty look.

"I didn't say I thought Enrique was guilty. I don't think he is. He was getting food for his sisters and trying to keep from getting shipped back to Mexico."

"We have to tell Cooper."

The phone rang just as Max started to pick it up. Cooper had seen the news as well, and we made plans to meet him the next day.

Max, as usual, went right to sleep, but I couldn't. My mind kept coming up with awful scenarios. With Enrique arrested, what was going to happen to the girls? I imagined them waiting on the island alone and hungry, worried about their older brother. I wasn't forgetting about the cougar either. Enrique had the boat, which meant they were stranded.

Assuming they were even on Ghost Island. Thinking about the island reminded me about Josh and Kevin. I felt better knowing that if the girls were stranded there, they might go in search of help. They'd find the archeologists' camp, and Josh and Kevin would be able to call . . . the police.

I tried to brush away the images from my mind, focusing instead on images my mother had shared with me in the early stages of my leukemia. "Just think about Jesus sitting beside you, gathering you in His arms—like He did the children in the Bible." I closed my eyes and imagined Callista and Maela sitting with Jesus. I prayed that no matter what happened, Jesus would be with them. I did the same for Enrique, praying that the real robbers would be found.

CHAPTER THIRTEEN

Morning came too soon, and with it news that Enrique would not tell the police where to find his sisters. He told them that he had never taken anything from any of the homes in Lakeside. Police had told the reporters that they had evidence to the contrary and they had made an arrest.

After breakfast, Amelia took us into town, saying she could get us in to talk with Enrique. The police officer Amelia talked to agreed to let us go in. Maybe he thought Enrique would talk to us since we were friends. "I don't know if he'll tell you anything," the officer said, "but the most important concern we have right now is locating those little girls. I don't think he realizes the danger they are in if we don't find them."

He took us into a visiting area where we sat at a table. Enrique had been crying and ducked his head when he saw us. "What do you want? Did the police send you? I'm not saying anything."

"Enrique, no. Just listen." I looked around, wondering if the police recorded conversations between prisoners and visitors. "We've been looking for you."

"Why? So you can get the reward?"

"Enrique, please." I lowered my voice. "We don't want you to be deported. We just want to help."

"She's right, buddy." Cooper leaned forward. "With you in here, Callista and Maela are in danger. Please tell us where they are. We can help you."

"They are strong. They can take care of themselves."

Max drummed her fingers on the surface of the table. "Please. Tell us where Callista and Maela are so we can at least bring them food and make sure they're safe."

"No. The police will arrest them too." Enrique looked worried, and I thought we might be breaking through. "Don't you understand? If I tell you anything, the police will follow you."

"We can make sure that doesn't happen."

"No." He leaned forward and whispered, "The spirits will guard them. I am not worried."

He jumped to his feet and slammed his fist onto the table.

I ducked, thinking he was going to hit one of us.

"You are not my friends." Enrique spat the words at me. "It's because of you the police caught me. You told them I had been at the market."

I wanted to deny it, but couldn't. My parents had apparently told the police what Sam and I had seen.

The guard grabbed Enrique. He scowled at the guard and said, "Take your hands off me. I can walk."

The guard ignored him and took him back to wherever they

were holding him. I held my hand to my throat, trying to make some sense out of what had just happened. An officer escorted us back out to where Amelia waited.

"Did he tell you anything?" Amelia asked.

"No." I glanced around at the clerk and another police officer, but couldn't be sure if they were listening to us. We walked straight out to Amelia's truck and climbed inside. Cooper jumped in the back with Amelia's dog, Molly.

Sitting between Max and Amelia, I felt my face grow warm with anger. "My parents must have told the police about Enrique getting food at the grocery store." I leaned back, wishing I could disappear into the seat. "It's their fault Enrique got caught. It's my fault for telling them."

Amelia shook her head. "Don't blame yourself, Jessie. I imagine the police have been waiting for activity on the water ever since Enrique and his sisters went missing. With that and the burglaries, I'm sure they would have caught him eventually. Did he tell you anything about the girls?"

I'm not sure, I started to say, then changed my mind. I felt certain he had given us a clue, but I had no intention of mentioning it to another adult—at least not until Cooper, Max, and I could discuss it. "I thought he might, but he just got really mad and started yelling. The guard took him away."

Nobody said much until we got back to the farm. I asked if I could stay over again. Amelia said yes if my parents agreed. Amelia asked us if we were okay with fish for dinner. We were.

Once we got back, I called my mom. I told her about Enrique. "I'm sorry, Jessie. We had no idea the police would try to charge him with the burglaries."

"Can I stay with Max again tonight?"

"Well, I . . ."

"Please."

She sighed heavily into the phone, and I had the feeling she was feeling some guilt herself. "All right, but call me in the morning."

"I will."

The three of us helped Amelia with dinner. While we ate salmon, rice, and salad greens from the garden, we talked about Enrique, his sisters, deportation, and the robberies.

"I can't believe Enrique was involved in any of those home robberies," Amelia said. "I believe you are right, Jessie. He's been too busy taking care of himself and his sisters to bother with stealing credit cards and electronic gadgets."

Cooper studied a piece of salmon before putting it in his mouth. "What if his aunt is really behind the robberies? She or one of her housekeepers worked at the places that were robbed. Didn't the police say she had keys to all those places?"

Max kicked him, and I glared at him from across the table. "How can you say that? Leah Estrada is a nice lady."

"Not only that," Amelia said, "but you don't build up a business based on trust and then start stealing from your clients."

"Maybe. But a lot of people seem nice, and then one day you find out they've been dealing drugs or robbing banks or killing people. What if she made Enrique steal for her? She might have been blackmailing him—like saying she'd turn him over to the immigration authorities if he didn't do what she said."

Max stood up and punched his arm. "Coop, I'm going to pretend I didn't hear that. I thought Enrique was your friend."

Cooper rubbed his arm. "He was—is. I don't know. The police don't arrest people without a reason. And his aunt has had all those keys."

"Circumstantial evidence," Amelia said. "It may be a coincidence. Leah Estrada has cleaned for me. I trust her. Now, it's possible that one of the women she has working for her is involved."

"Yeah." Cooper brightened. "Like Mrs. Dougherty."

"As in Sunny's mother?" I dropped my fork. "She works for Leah?"

Cooper nodded. "My dad uses Leah's maid service. We have a homemaker come in twice a week to clean and cook. When we got home from Seattle, Sunny's mother was there cleaning. I was going to tell you, but with everything else going on, I didn't get a chance."

"So did she say anything?" Max asked. "Like why does she need to clean houses? They live in a mansion."

He shrugged. "I went upstairs to work on my new laptop. All I know is that they talked for about two hours. I saw her leave, but Dad wouldn't tell me anything when I asked. He and my mom and Sunny's parents were friends before my mother . . ." He choked up and I looked away.

Amelia patted Cooper's shoulder and started clearing our

plates. "I can answer at least some of your questions. The Doughertys have been having some financial problems. They're selling their house because they have no choice. And I imagine Catherine Dougherty has no choice but to work now that her husband is out of the picture."

"What do you mean?" I carried my dishes to the sink. "He didn't die, did he?"

"No. I think death would have been easier. Chad Dougherty left and filed for divorce."

"Oh." I sighed. "Not that it's any excuse, but that sure explains Sunny's attitude."

Max pursed her lips. "Maybe Mrs. Dougherty is behind the thefts. Sounds like she could use the money."

"I seriously doubt she would resort to stealing," Amelia said. "Though I don't like to blame the tourists for everything, I have a hard time seeing our neighbors as thieves."

"I hope you're right," Cooper said.

After dinner we did the dishes while Amelia went into the living room to put her feet up and relax. By the time we'd finished, she'd fallen asleep in her recliner. Max left her a note saying we were going out on the lake for a little while and would be back before dark.

"I've been thinking about our visit with Enrique," I said as I slipped a life jacket over my head.

"Me too." Cooper blew out a long breath. "I've never seen him get mad at anybody."

"Well, I can't believe he wouldn't tell us where his sisters are." Max got into the canoe, and I climbed in after her.

"I think he did tell us." I gripped the sides of the canoe while Cooper got in and shoved off.

"What are you talking about? He basically told us to mind our own business."

"That was for show," I said. "Remember when he said, '*The spirits will guard them*'?"

Max repeated the words Enrique had whispered to us just before he went ballistic.

"It can only mean one thing," I said. "We've been right all along. They've been hiding on Ghost Island."

"But where?" Cooper asked. "It isn't like we haven't looked."

"We only rowed around it," Max said. "We didn't actually go on the island except for near the archeology camp."

"Yeah." Cooper rested the oar on his lap. "But you're forgetting—the island is off-limits."

"You're right." I dangled my hand in the water and watched the droplets come off my fingers. "Maybe we need to tell the police that the girls might be on the island."

Max reached for the oar and directed the canoe farther from shore. "We can't do that, Jess. I vote we go out to the island right now and have another look around. Maybe have another talk with Josh and Kevin."

"It can't hurt," Cooper agreed.

"I think it's a bad idea. It's getting late and . . ."

"That's just it. We need to go now. Maela and Callista have already been out there alone for one night. We can't let them be out there for another one. Don't forget about the cougar. We have to at least try. They're probably hungry and scared. If I were them, I'd want someone like us to find them. We could take them to Lakeside Farm. Mrs. T would keep them hidden and maybe even find a way for them to stay in the U.S."

Max's reasons were full of flaws, but I heard myself agreeing. "Okay," I said, "but we told Amelia we'd be back before dark. It's already almost seven. That doesn't give us much time." I had a bad feeling about this. It wasn't just that we hadn't asked permission; it was also because we were in the canoe instead of the rowboat. And the dark storm clouds hovering near the island didn't ease my worries at all.

"We have over an hour, and we're halfway there." Max paddled faster. "Besides, you guys have your cell phones, don't you? If we run into trouble, you can call for help."

Cooper and I checked our phones to make sure they were charged.

He dropped his cell into his pocket, and mine went into my bag. "Let's row to the place Maela's float toy came from." He pointed to a spot on the island where we could see an outcropping of rocks. We'd had to weave around them when we navigated the island the other day.

We were about a football field away from the island when the wind came up. Those dark clouds I'd seen earlier had moved in to block what was left of the sun. A drop of rain hit my nose, and two more splattered on my cheek. I looked up into the darkening sky and cringed. Lightning flashed, and seconds later thunder rumbled and exploded around us. The canoe shifted back and forth on the wind-roughened water. I gripped the sides of the canoe. "We have to go back."

"I don't think so." Cooper seemed extremely calm as he reached for the oar. "I'll row us to the island. We need to get off the lake." The raindrops came harder and faster. More lightning, and thunder that sounded like we were in the middle of a battlefield.

As Max rose off her seat to hand Cooper the oar, the canoe smacked into a rock. Max screamed. The oar flew from her hand. She spread out her arms to steady herself, but the canoe tipped wildly from side to side. Max toppled into the lake.

"Max!" I screamed. She should have bounced up and grabbed the canoe. But she didn't. I stared at the place she'd fallen in but saw nothing except the dark, murky water. It didn't help that she wasn't wearing a life jacket. Max usually wore a life belt under her shirt. At least I think she did. I couldn't remember seeing her put it on.

CHAPTER FOURTEEN

Cooper knelt beside me. "She must have hit her head on the rocks. I'm going in." Cooper pulled off his sneakers and rolled over the side of the boat into the water. He thrashed around the boat for what seemed like forever. Finally, he came up gasping for air. "I've got her."

"Is she okay?"

"Don't know . . . I think so . . . There are some rocks here. I'm going to try to get her into the canoe. You pull and I'll try to lift her."

Cooper lifted her limp body partway into the boat. I got my hands under her arms and pulled hard. "She's too heavy . . ." I grunted. "I can't pull her in."

"Okay, hold on to her, Jess. I'll get in." Cooper's weight along with Max's pulled the boat over. I lost my grip on Max and fell backward into the freezing water. I started thrashing around, trying not to panic. I needed to get to the surface. *Stay calm. You'll float. You have on a life jacket.* My hand scraped against rocks and sand. I turned and pushed off when my feet settled on the bottom.

By the time I reached the surface, my lungs felt like they were going to explode. I tipped my head back and grabbed a gallon of air.

"Cooper! Max!" I couldn't see them or the canoe. I couldn't see anything except giant shadows of trees against the ugly rain-soaked sky. I called again. No answer. Had Cooper been able to get Max to shore? Cooper had his life jacket on too.

Lightning lit up the island for one brief moment—long enough for me to see the ragged shoreline. Then darkness again. I began doing a breaststroke.

I'd only gone a few feet when my knee snagged against a rock. I was able to stand on it and catch my breath, but only for a minute. Cooper was right—we needed to get out of the water. A lightning strike in the right place could fry us. I could only hope that he and Max had already made it to shore.

I don't know how long it took me to make land. A lot longer than it should have. Even with the life jacket, I'd had to paddle hard to keep from losing ground against the current. I dragged myself up onto a rock ledge and lay there until my breathing returned to normal. The rock still had a little warmth in it from a day full of sunshine. I turned over on my back. The rain had stopped, but the night sky offered no light. No moon. No stars.

I made myself believe that Cooper and Max had made it to shore not far from where I was. That Max was awake and strong as ever. Cooper would have dragged Max to shore. Even with the load, he would have gotten there a lot faster than me. The current must have dragged me farther south, closer to the archeology camp.

I couldn't believe it. Stranded. Again. I should have stayed behind. Soaking wet and with no boat, we were no good at all to Maela and Callista—assuming they were here in the first place.

The garbled thoughts swam through my mind as I lay there wondering what to do next. Cooper's and my cell phones were probably lying at the bottom of the lake. Mom and Dad would not be happy that I'd lost another one. Amelia would have called them by now. They'd all be worried. Would they know to come here? Probably not, but it's one of the first places they'd check, right?

I rolled onto my side, curling up to ward off the chilling dampness. The shivering seemed to come from inside of me and wouldn't stop. I had to get warm. I thought about Josh and Kevin's camp. Maybe they'd have a campfire. At least they'd have dry clothes. I jumped up and down and hugged myself in an attempt to get my blood circulating. I couldn't remember ever being this cold.

Okay, Jessie, you need to think, I told myself. *The island is not that big. If you walk close to the shoreline, you'll eventually get to the camp.* Then I remembered the cliff we'd seen when we entered the camp. I'd never be able to get around it. Looking into the inky black forest made me shiver even more. An owl hooted as if to warn me of the dangers of wandering through the woods at night. Not that I needed a warning. If Josh and Kevin were right, I'd be sharing the woods with a cougar.

The storm had passed and I could now see some stars. Since the rain had stopped, I could see the lights of the towns in the distance. Off to my right were the lights of Lakeside Farm. I tried to orient myself to where on the island I had come ashore and where Cooper and Max might be.

I honestly didn't know what to do. If you get lost, you're supposed to stay put and let people find you. Ordinarily I would have, but I had to find the camp. I didn't know how badly Max had been hurt. What if she needed medical attention? Josh and Kevin would have flashlights. They also had a boat and could take us back to the mainland.

I suppose it might have been smarter to wait until morning, but I felt like I had to do something right away. I pictured maps I'd seen of Ghost Island. Cutting through the forest seemed the most logical thing to do. I'd keep the large rock formation to my right and eventually I'd get to the archeology camp.

I took several deep breaths and began walking—or stumbling. Old-growth forest was not as thick as planted forests, but the ground was uneven and strewn with moss-covered logs and rotting tree limbs. In the daytime the forest might have been fun to explore, but at night it was like wandering through a terrifying Halloween movie. Branches waved and reached out to grab me. Roots rose out of the ground like tentacles. As I moved forward, I kept waving my arms to the front and side to keep from running headfirst into a tree. I recited lines from the 23rd Psalm. *The Lord is my shepherd . . . though I walk through the valley of the shadow of death I will fear no evil . . . I will fear no evil.*

I stopped beside a fallen tree to catch my breath. In the stillness I thought I heard voices. Then I saw a light through the trees some ways away—a flickering campfire. It had to be the archeology camp.

I got up and walked a little faster. I could see the campfire more clearly now, but something didn't feel right. My first inclination had been to run into the camp. Now I held back. Clumps of vine maple provided good cover. I crouched down and waited for my eyes to grow accustomed to the light.

"This will have to be the last load," Kevin was saying. "We won't be coming back."

"What do we do with the kids?" Josh poked a stick into the fire, stirring up the embers.

"Leave them here. I'm not taking them along. We can call the cops to come and pick them up."

What kids? Callista and Maela? Max and Cooper?

"I don't like it." Josh rubbed the back of his head as he paced back and forth in front of the fire.

"We don't have a choice." Kevin sounded angry. "We can't risk the cops coming out here and finding the stash."

It suddenly hit me that Josh and Kevin were up to more than digging through ancient ruins. They were behind the robberies. I didn't want to believe it. They had seemed like such nice guys.

Kevin glanced over at the tent. "They'll be all right. They might be able to tell about the camp, but I'm not worried about that. Besides, who's going to believe them? The cops will think they're just protecting their brother."

"Yeah. It was a stroke of genius sticking that jewelry in the Mexican kid's boat and calling the cops with that tip."

I didn't feel cold anymore. I was too angry. How I ever thought these guys were cool, I'll never know. Only now that I knew they were thieves, what could I do about it? I couldn't run out and confront them. And I had no way of letting anyone know what I'd learned.

"We'd better start packing up." Kevin got up and stretched.

"I'm ready to go. I'll start carrying our stash to the boat."

I stayed crouched behind the maple. If they were both loading their boat, maybe I could get to the girls and release them. I wished Max and Cooper were here.

I'd no sooner thought about them than I heard Max's cheerful voice. "Hey, guys. I was hoping you'd be here. We need help."

Oh, no. I held my breath as I watched Cooper and Max come closer to the fire. "My canoe capsized and I . . ." Max must have seen Callista and Maela in the tent. "Hey, what's going on?"

They didn't have a chance. Even though they turned to run, Josh and Kevin were on them in less than five seconds. As much as I wanted to jump in and save them, I knew I'd be no match for them. The best I could do was wait and set Cooper and Max free when the guys were loading their boat.

Josh and Kevin tied up Cooper and Max. The way Max was

fighting, I knew without a doubt she'd recovered from the canoe accident.

"Now what?" Josh stepped away from Cooper and brushed off his hands. "We can't leave these kids here. They'll tell the cops on us for sure."

"It's their own fault for trespassing on the island in the first place." Kevin drew a gun. "Looks like we have two choices. I shoot them here and now or we'll have to take them out with us. Dump them out in the lake—and drown them."

Josh sat down and covered his face. "They're just kids, Kevin. It wasn't supposed to go down like this."

Kevin ran a hand through his hair. "We don't have a choice."

They were not going to get rid of Max and Cooper. I might not be strong enough to fight them, but I knew exactly what I had to do.

CHAPTER FIFTEEN

I went back into the woods and, staying under cover, made my way to the back of the outhouse and around to the dock. The archeologists, if that's what they really were, couldn't see me from there. There were two boats now: the rowboat and a larger motorboat with a cabin below deck. They must have needed a bigger boat to carry their stash.

I released the ropes from the cleats and pushed both boats out into the water. They drifted a few feet and stopped. That wasn't going to help at all. Somehow I had to get them out into the current and set them adrift. I waded out to the rowboat and climbed into it, then rowed up to the cabin cruiser. I grabbed the rope that dangled from the prow and tied it to the back of the rowboat. Grasping the oars, I rowed as hard as I could. I only rowed a few feet before I caught the current.

Even so, my arms and hands started hurting, but I was doing it. I stayed close to shore and soon the dock disappeared from view. I could tell when I was in the current as both boats began to move without my rowing. I untied the bigger boat and began rowing back. As soon as I neared the dock, I got out of the rowboat. The water was hip deep and hidden from the camp. I tipped the boat to the side, letting it fill with water. As I stepped onto the rocks, footsteps sounded on the dock. "Hey," Josh yelled. "Where are the boats?"

I knew he couldn't see me, but I still jumped.

Kevin came running down to join him. I could hear them swearing and blaming each other for not tying up the boats. One of them jumped into the water. I hoped by now the cabin cruiser was too far away for them to catch. A good swimmer might be able to reach it.

I hurried back to the camp and released Cooper and Max, who helped me with the girls. Since cell phones were listed among the burglarized items, I figured there might still be one in their camp in one of the boxes that sat packed and ready to go. Cooper found one, but we didn't have time to make a call.

"They're coming after us," I cried, seeing the flashlight beams bouncing toward us. "We have to hurry."

"We'd better hold on to each other," Cooper said.

Callista's hand closed around mine and pulled me to the left. "This way."

Cooper lifted Maela onto his back and took my hand, and Max took up the rear.

We moved slowly and cautiously under cover of the trees and shrubs.

I could hear Josh and Kevin yelling at each other. “We can’t let them get away.”

“Let’s split up. They can’t get far.”

“They must have a boat stashed on the other side.” Josh couldn’t have been more than ten feet away. He trained his flashlight in our direction.

We dropped to the ground, hoping the vine maple and fallen trees would cover us. The beam traveled over our heads. I closed my eyes and prayed they wouldn’t see us. The musty smell of moss and earth made me want to sneeze. I pinched my nose tight and held my breath.

A low-pitched growl came from the bushes behind me, sending my heart into overdrive.

Josh must have heard it too, because he whipped around and started running in the opposite direction. “Did you hear that?” he yelped. “I’m getting my gun.”

“W-what was that?” I managed to get the words past my tight throat once he’d gone.

Max brushed herself off and in hushed tones said. “M-maybe we’d better take our chances with Josh and Kevin.”

“Sounded like a cougar.” Cooper, with Maela still attached to his back, struggled to get up.

Maela giggled. “Not a cougar, silly. That was Callista.”

“Callista?”

“Shh. Come. We are not safe here.” We joined hands again and continued to follow her.

"Where are we going?" I whispered.

"It's not far."

We reached what had to be the rock wall and followed it a short distance before it curved inward. I tried to imagine what it might look like in the daylight. Following the curve, we backtracked several feet. Callista stopped. "We must climb this steep hill. There is a ledge and a cave where we will be safe."

After what seemed like forever, we reached the ledge Callista had mentioned and rested. A few minutes later, Callista led us back into a cave. At least that's what she called it. It was still too dark to see anything. Maybe that was a good thing. The moon might have helped us to see better, but it would have given Josh and Kevin better light as well.

Callista appeared at my side with a small flashlight. "Don't worry," she said. "They won't be able to see the light from out there. We can hear them if they climb on the rocks."

Cooper pulled out the cell phone and tried to call for help. "There's no signal in here." He went outside to try, but after a few minutes, he gave up. "When it's light, I'll climb up higher and see if I can get through." He crossed his legs and dropped to the ground looking almost as wiped out as I felt.

We had a lot to talk about, but that could wait. The escape had left me exhausted. I started shaking—maybe from my clothes still being damp, or from being totally worn out. The fact that I had managed to come this far was a miracle.

"Maela," Callista said. "Come." They disappeared into an even darker cavity and minutes later returned with clothes, blankets, and some food. "Here are some of Enrique's clothes. Jessie, I have a sweater that might fit you. It is not much, but the blankets should warm you."

We thanked her and took turns going back into the cave to change. My lightweight cotton pants had almost dried, so I just took off my soggy sweatshirt and put on Callista's sweater. Once we'd changed and wrapped ourselves in blankets, we sat in a circle around a rock-encircled fire pit, but there'd be no fire tonight.

Maela pressed herself against Callista and stared at us through drooping eyes.

Callista pulled her little sister close. "Please, tell us about Enrique. Those men told us he had been arrested for stealing."

"He's in detention," Cooper said. "But he won't stay there. We'll tell the police what really happened as soon as we can call out."

"How did you end up in their camp, Callista?" I asked.

Callista shifted slightly and lowered Maela's head onto her lap. "When Enrique didn't come back, we waited here all night. We grew worried. Maela and I went to the place where he keeps the boat, but it was still gone. On the way back the men found us. They took us to their camp. I don't know how they knew we were here. We were very quiet."

"That may have been our fault," I said. "We came out here a few days ago, right after you ran away, and we asked Josh and Kevin if they had seen you."

"But we didn't know they were crooks." Max rubbed her head and winced.

"Max, you're hurt." I reached for her.

She waved my hand away. "I hit my head on the rocks. Knocked me out for a while."

"Which reminds me, Jessie," Cooper said. "What happened to you?"

"You're the ones who disappeared. I called and you didn't answer. I was afraid you'd both drowned."

"It was tough getting Max to shore. I went under a few times. Maybe you just yelled at the wrong time. I thought you were right behind me. We waited for a while, but when you didn't come, we thought we'd better go looking for you."

"I got caught in the current. It took me forever to get to shore, and when I did I wasn't sure what to do. I thought you guys might try to get to the archeology camp for help, so that's where I went."

"You were right. We were going to ask them to help find you since they had flashlights and stuff."

"Big mistake." Max sighed. "I can't believe I just barged into their camp. When I saw Callista and Maela all tied up, it was too late to do anything."

"I'm just glad you weren't with us, Jess," Cooper said. "By the way, thanks for saving our necks."

"Don't thank me yet. We're still stuck on the island with these guys. Maybe I shouldn't have sabotaged their boats. At least they'd have been able to leave."

"If they had, we might never be able to prove that Enrique isn't behind the robberies."

"I wonder if Mrs. T knows we're missing yet." Max sounded doubtful. "Sometimes when she falls asleep in her recliner she sleeps all night."

"Which means no one will know we're missing until morning." I thought I heard the shattering of rock just outside. Had Josh and Kevin found us? I reached for the flashlight and shut it off. "Listen."

There it was again. Only this time when I heard the low throaty growl, I knew it wasn't Callista.

"Oh, man," Cooper moaned. "It's the cougar."

CHAPTER SIXTEEN

I froze as a pair of yellow eyes floated into the cave. Weird and scary.

"Give me the flashlight." Cooper slowly got to his feet.

I handed him the light and he turned it on, shining the beam directly into the big cat's eyes. Cooper waved his arms. "Shoo! Scat!"

The cougar didn't move, but he seemed even more scary now that I could see the eyes attached to his body. *His long, sleek, powerful body.*

He's more afraid of you than you are of him, I reminded myself. At the moment, I wasn't so sure about that. I hoped he wouldn't attack, because I couldn't have moved my feet if someone started a fire under me.

"If we make a lot of noise, maybe we can scare him." Cooper jiggled the light.

"If we make a lot of noise," I whispered, "Josh and Kevin might hear us."

"I . . ." Max took a step back. "I'd rather take our chances with the cat. At least he doesn't have a gun. And he can't attack all of us at once."

"I think he is just curious." Callista woke Maela and got to her feet. "Maybe if we stay very still he'll go away."

"Do you think this is his den?" I asked.

"He's never been in here before." Callista bit her lower lip. "At least not that we know of."

"Okay, listen." Cooper kept the flashlight beam trained on the cat. "I'm going to shine the light right in his eyes. Then I'll shut it off. Max, you grab Maela and pull her back. Do it fast."

"No, Cooper," Callista said. "A sudden movement might cause him to attack."

The growling stopped. The cougar looked at each one of us as if checking out food on a buffet table. I guess none of us looked all that appetizing, because he turned around and walked out. Just like that.

"Amazing." Max kept her eyes on the opening. "He didn't seem afraid. Or dangerous."

Cooper sat down. "He's smart. Probably sized us up and decided not to challenge us."

I had to sit down too, as I didn't think my spaghetti legs would hold me up. I hauled in a shaky breath. "Do you think he'll come back?"

Cooper shrugged. "I don't know. One thing for sure—I'm not about to leave the cave to look for him."

"We better take turns keeping watch," Max said. "In case he

comes back. I'm too wired to sleep now anyway, so I'll go first."

"Okay." Cooper yawned and leaned against the rock wall near the opening. "Wake me up in an hour."

"I'll go after Cooper." I pulled the blanket around me and curled up on the cave floor. I know it sounds strange, but I felt safe somehow. At least safer than I had since we'd left Lakeside Farm over six hours ago.

Sunlight filtered into the cave. Our night visitor hadn't come back. At least I don't think he had. I rubbed my eyes and glanced around at all the sleeping forms. So much for keeping watch. Neither Cooper nor Max had moved since I fell asleep. A quick check assured me that yes, they were all just sleeping and our cougar hadn't decided to have any of them for breakfast.

I captured the cell phone from Cooper's side and took it outside. My watch told me it was only 6:00 a.m. Looking around, I noticed we were about midway up the rocky cliff that stood guard over the archeologist's camp. I ducked out of sight when I saw the tent. Thankfully, the ledge was wide enough to hide the entrance to the cave. I checked the cell phone, but with the rock wall separating us from the populated side of the lake, I couldn't get a signal.

"Cool." Max sat down beside me. "We can see right into their camp."

"So far I haven't seen them moving around. They probably gave up on finding us last night."

"Can you get a signal?"

I shook my head. "We probably need to get on the other side of this hill. Or go down closer to the dock."

"I'll do it." Cooper came up behind me. "Give me the phone."

"It might be too late." Max pointed out toward the water. "There's a cabin cruiser coming this way. And I don't think it's the cops."

"Maybe it's their professor," I said, handing the phone to Cooper. "The way Josh and Kevin talked, they weren't in on this scam alone."

"They must have called him last night," Max said.

"Look, whoever it is found the boat I released last night. They're going to get away after all."

"At least you slowed them down." Max lay on her stomach and peered over the edge. "I wish we had the binoculars. I can't make out the face. We need to get closer."

"No, we don't." I grabbed Max's arm. "It's too dangerous. Cooper will make the phone call, and then we wait until the police come."

"I'm on it." Cooper started down the trail. "I'll untie the boats if I can."

"Be careful," I warned. "Those guys don't want to leave any witnesses behind."

"I don't think we should let Coop go down there alone." Max scowled.

"Max, look." Two people disembarked the boat, and one of them was Sunny Dougherty.

CHAPTER SEVENTEEN

"Um—I could be wrong, but I don't think she's too happy about being here."

"Jess, Sunny isn't happy about being anywhere."

"Seriously. Look at how that guy is holding her arm. She's trying to get away from him."

"We've got to get closer. I want to hear what they're saying."

"We can't take the chance. If we start down that trail, they'll see us." When I turned toward Max, she was already heading down the hill. I didn't have much choice but to follow her.

I told Callista and Maela to stay inside the cave and that we'd be back as soon as we could.

How we made it all the way down the hill without being detected, I'll never know. Max was waiting for me when I got to the bottom. We stayed close to the rock wall and reached the clearing in a few minutes. Apparently, Josh and Kevin had gone down to meet the boat, as they were all coming back when Max and I took cover behind the vine maple.

"That guy is Sunny's brother, Jason," I whispered.

Jason pushed his sister ahead of him. "Sit down over there and shut up. I'm tired of your whining."

"You'll be sorry."

"I already am." To Josh and Kevin, he said, "I can't believe you guys couldn't take care of a couple bratty kids. And then to let them set your boats adrift."

"What about you, bringing your little sister?"

"I told you before—she was snooping around and figured out what I was doing."

"What are we going to do now?" Kevin asked. "We can't let all these kids stay here on the island, and we can't take them with us. I sure don't want to shoot them. We don't have time to go looking for them."

Sunny folded her arms. "I could cover for you."

"What are you talking about?"

"You're getting a lot of money out of this, aren't you? Give me a share and I'll make sure you get away."

I wondered how Sunny planned on doing that. These guys were crazy to think they'd get away with their crimes.

"I'll tell the police it was Enrique. You'll still be the innocent archeology students from the U. You'll still have the perfect scam."

"What makes you think they'll believe you over your friends?"

"They are not my friends." Sunny stood up taller. "Think about it. Cooper is Enrique's best friend. Jessie and Max are going to go along with whatever Cooper says. No one will believe them. The police already have Enrique in custody. They think his aunt gave him the keys. Trust me, I'm not going to say anything about how you duplicated Mom's keys."

Max stiffened. "I'm going to get that lying, backstabbing maggot."

"Max." I grabbed her arm. "Stay down."

She clenched her fists, but stayed put.

Sunny started laughing and pointing toward the water. "Don't look now, guys, but your boats are leaving without you."

Sure enough, Cooper had untied both vessels. One must have had a key in it because he started it up, put it in gear, and took off.

The three men raced for the boat dock. Jason took off his shoes and dove in.

Sunny turned toward us, her smile gone. "You might be able to fool those dorks, Max, but you can't fool me. I can smell you a mile away." She walked right into the bushes where we were hiding.

Max stood up, hands on her hips. "What are you gonna do, sic your big brother on us?"

"Max . . ." I put a restraining hand on her arm. I could tell by the look of fear on Sunny's face and the tears in her eyes that she was terrified.

"Help me." All the fight seemed to have drained out her. "They aren't going to let me just stay here. I know too much, and you do too."

"Come on." Max and I led Sunny to the cave. We had no idea what Josh and his friends would do if they caught us. Cooper must have gotten hold of the police by now, if not with the cell phone, then definitely with the radio on the boat. I just didn't know how long it would take for them to get here. From the ledge, we couldn't see anything except the camp and the boat dock. The guys were gone and I had no idea where. If they had taken time to explore the island, they might know about the cave and suspect that we'd be here.

"Thanks." Sunny sat down on the ledge with her back against the stone wall. "I didn't really plan to take their money. I had to think of some way to keep them from killing me."

"Do you seriously think Jason would hurt you?"

She closed her eyes. "He wouldn't have before, but he's been doing drugs. These thefts were to make money for his habit. I didn't think Jason would ever hurt me, but when he made me go with him on the boat . . ." She swallowed. "I was so scared."

"There are too many of us now," Max said. "And the cops should be here any minute. We'll testify and it will be all over."

"My mother didn't have anything to do with this." Sunny frowned.

"I know. We heard what you said about your brother making keys."

"It was stupid." Sunny put a finger through a small hole in her jeans and ripped it even more.

We heard the sirens before we saw the patrol boat pull into the dock. I looked around for the three men, but still saw no sign of them. I just hoped they wouldn't be running in our direction.

When everything that can go wrong does go wrong, my mother says it's Murphy's Law. We were starting to feel safe when we heard the rocks skittering down the hill just outside the cave.

"Up here," one of the guys yelled. "There's a cave." They were on the trail below us. I wasn't about to give up without a fight. Max and I looked at each other and at the rocks and started picking up the larger ones. Sunny caught on right away. We signaled for Callista and Maela to stay inside the cave.

The moment Kevin's head appeared over the rock promontory we started pitching the rocks.

"Head for cover!" He ducked.

"Ouch."

"Go back down."

"I can't."

"Why not?"

"The mountain lion is blocking our way."

I never did figure out who said what, but I'll never forget that moment or the minutes that followed.

"So are the police!" a woman yelled. "Hands on your heads."

Bam! The deafening gunshot silenced the men, the cougar, and all of us.

We could hear the police leading the thieves down the hill. Less than a minute later, two deputies came up to get us. We reached the camp just in time to see the three cuffed fugitives being boarded onto the sheriff's cabin cruiser. Cooper was waiting on the dock with another officer.

Cooper had told them where to find us, and they'd arrived just in time. Max and Sunny both insisted that we could have fought the guys off, but I wasn't so sure. Thanks to a few well-placed rocks, the cougar, and the cops, we were safely heading back to Chenoa Lake.

On the way, the sheriff called our parents and told them we'd be at the police station. It took a while for all of us to tell our versions of what had happened. My parents took me home, and I didn't even get a lecture. Mom and Dad were just happy that we'd escaped safely. As it turned out, they didn't even know we were missing until that morning when Cooper's dad, Amelia, and my parents compared notes and realized we had been gone all night.

The next day, Max and Cooper came over to debrief. Of course, we had to go to the Alpine Tea and Candy Shoppe for strawberries and scones. The minute we walked in, Ivy seated us and apologized over and over for what Sunny had done at the swimming pool. "I had no idea she was going to take your clothes. I just want you to know that I no longer consider her a friend. No way."

I was glad to hear that and also pleased that Ivy would side herself with Max, Cooper, and me.

The debriefing took several twists and turns. Just like this case had. First came Cooper's tirade over Sunny taking credit for capturing the thieves. "Just look at this article. Front page. Sunny got an interview with a reporter and makes it sound like *she* called the police and *she* uncovered the real story. We aren't mentioned in the article at all except that *she* helped the police rescue the five children being held captive on Ghost Island by the phony archeologists."

"Why would she do that?" Max studied the article and turned away in disgust. "I was just beginning to think she was okay."

"I wouldn't let it get to me." I broke off a small piece of lavender blueberry scone. "We know what really happened out there. So do the people that really matter. Besides, Sunny did figure out what her brother was up to. And she did tell the police the truth about him. Maybe Sunny needs to feel important. She must be feeling embarrassed about her brother."

"That makes sense," Cooper said. "But what really worries me is that . . ." He looked away.

"What?" Max elbowed him. "Coop, you look like you just lost your hard drive."

"Worse." He sighed. "My dad is taking Sunny's mother to the concert tonight. Do you realize what that means? If he really likes her and she really likes him, they might get married, and Sunny would be my . . . my . . . I can't say it."

"Sister." Max pretended to gag.

"Poor Cooper." I patted his shoulder.

"Look at it this way," Ivy said. "Sunny will be going off to college in another—" she gulped "—six years. Well, at least Mrs. Dougherty is a really nice lady."

Just so you don't think this story ends on a totally depressing note, I should tell you the good news. Enrique and his sisters won't be deported after all. It seems that the immigration department found that Carlos had never been an illegal. His killer had apparently destroyed his green card and papers and spread the rumor that he had left the area. Leah had been right about him, but the authorities took forever to find Carlos in the system. He had applied for U.S. citizenship before he had died. He just hadn't told anyone. The papers granting him and his underage children U.S. citizenship had been processed and were still in the system, waiting. Enrique and his sisters would be staying with Leah Estrada for good.

As for the cougar, a team from the Fish & Wildlife Department shot him with a tranquilizing gun and took him to the mainland on the opposite side of the lake. There he'd have plenty of deer and rabbits to eat.

When I got back home, Dad was waiting for me. With the fishing poles all set up and a lunch packed, I had a feeling this was going to be a l-o-n-g day with one of those l-o-n-g talks about the subjects parents feel they need to talk about.

I smiled as I climbed into the boat and waved at Mom and Sam. "What's the topic for today, Dad?" I reached for the oars and he raised an eyebrow.

"I think I'll let you choose." He leaned back, with his hands behind his neck and legs stretched out.

At that moment, I loved my dad more than all the chocolate-dipped strawberries in the world. And I hoped God would give me lots more time to spend with him, my mom, Sam, and my friends.

ACKNOWLEDGMENTS

Thanks to my writer friends for their critique, support, and encouragement. And to Jan Bono and Birdie Etchison who helped me brainstorm Ghost Island and all its secrets.

ABOUT THE AUTHOR

Internationally known author and speaker **Patricia H. Rushford** has book sales totaling over a million copies. She has written numerous articles and authored over forty books, including *What Kids Need Most in a Mom, Have You Hugged Your Teenager Today?,* and *It Shouldn't Hurt to be a Kid.* She also writes a number of mystery series: *The Jennie McGrady Mysteries* for kids and the *Helen Bradley Mysteries* for adults. Her latest releases include: *The McAllister Files, She Who Watches, The Angel Delaney Mysteries* with *As Good as Dead* and a romantic suspense, *Sins of the Mother.* Her newest series for children is *The Max & Me Mysteries.*

One of her mysteries, *Silent Witness,* was nominated for an Edgar by Mystery Writers of America and won the Silver Angel for excellence in media. *Betrayed* was selected as best mystery for young adults *The Oregonian* (1997) and won the Phantom Friends Award. *Morningsong,* a romantic suspense, won the Golden Quill for Inspirational Romance award.

Patricia is a registered nurse and holds a Master's Degree in Counseling. In addition, she conducts writers workshops for adults and children and is codirector of *Writer's Weekend at the Beach.* She is the current director of the Oregon Christian Writers Summer Conference. Pat has appeared on numerous radio and television talk shows across the U.S. and Canada. She lives in the Portland, Oregon, area with her husband.

www.patriciarushford.com
Author/Speaker
What Kids Need Most in a Mom
The Jennie Mcgrady Mysteries
The McAllister Files
The Angel Delaney Mysteries
The Helen Bradley Mysteries
The Max & Me Mysteries (New!)